SMILE OF A STRANGER

When Ruth Stafford joins her mother at the Sea Winds Hotel, she has misgivings about Cecily Stafford's imminent marriage to Willard Enderby. Ruth suspects he has designs on her mother's recent legacy. If so, she is determined to unmask him! She is helped by another hotel guest, and finds herself falling deeply in love with him ... but is this endearing stranger any more trustworthy than Willard? Joys, heartbreaks and divided loyalties lie ahead before her questions find answers.

MAVIS THOMAS

SMILE OF A STRANGER

Complete and Unabridged

LINFORD
Leicester

First published in Great Britain in 2007

First Linford Edition
published 2008

British Library CIP Data

Thomas, Mavis
    Smile of a stranger.—Large print ed.—
Linford romance library
    1. Fortune hunters—Fiction 2. Mothers and
daughters—Fiction 3. Love stories
    4. Large type books
    I. Title
    823.9'2 [F]

    ISBN 978–1–84782–299–4

Published by
F. A. Thorpe (Publishing)
Anstey, Leicestershire

Set by Words & Graphics Ltd.
Anstey, Leicestershire
Printed and bound in Great Britain by
T. J. International Ltd., Padstow, Cornwall

This book is printed on acid-free paper

1

'Whitedene Bay! This is Whitedene Bay!' a metallic voice boomed. 'Passengers for Brighton, please change to Platform Three!'

Doors slid open. The length of the train shimmered with heat on this fine midsummer evening.

Some of the travellers were London commuters, thankfully returning with their briefcases and newspapers. Some were holiday people, supervising luggage. On the opposite platform, sunburnt day-trippers waited with weary, fretful children.

I fitted into none of these categories. Even though I was here straight from my daily stint of computer screen and telephone and an irascible Mr. Harding requiring the Architect's report ready before the meeting: even though a quite impressive label, *Sea Winds Hotel,*

Lower Beach Parade, graced the luggage I humped on to the platform. For me, this was no holiday. I was here on an errand of duty, a major task that no-one else would do — because no-one else seemed to believe it needed doing at all.

'Ruth! — Ruthie, I'm here!' My mother's eager voice hailed me before I reached the ticket barrier. 'You did catch the train, then!'

'Only just, Mum. Mr. Harding was breathing fire.'

'Well, just let him breathe it! How are you, dear? . . . How's Nina? . . . How's Alan? . . .'

Anyone might have thought we had been apart months instead of days. But this rapturous greeting was just her way. Excitement flushed her prettily small-featured face that wouldn't be misplaced on a treasured Victorian doll. With the still unfaded light-gold hair (just complemented by discreet 'rinses' at Lyn's Crop-'n'-Curl Salon) highlighting those cornflower blue eyes I found it hard to remember she was well into her late fifties. You couldn't think of age in the presence of Cecily Stafford.

'We can get a taxi outside,' she hustled me. 'Such a shame your car went and died on you! — can Alan get it fixed while you're here? . . . I can't wait to show you the hotel! — and you're having such a nice room, dear Will arranged it specially! He went off this morning on some dreary business thing or he'd be here too to meet you. It was such a wonderful idea of yours to come and stay here with us, we both thought so!'

'Was he really pleased, when I rang to say I was coming?'

'Of course! He can't be all the time with me, he has his work to do. I'm never quite sure what a 'Finance Consultant' does, but he goes to meetings, sees lots of people, he works very hard. We both want you to have a lovely holiday!'

'I hope I shall,' I said soberly. I bent my head for her warm kiss.

Outside, where cars and taxis lined the station approach, a driver came forward for my luggage. She told him importantly, 'Sea Winds, please — on the Lower Beach.' To me she added, 'It's not big and showy but it's the best! — dear Will always knows just what he's doing!'

I said nothing, unwilling to mar already her joy of reunion. I let her chatter on while we were ferried through the town centre, peopled by summer-clad loiterers around souvenir shops and cafes. Deck-chairs still lined a red-paved promenade, children splashed at the water's calm edge. The world of holiday was strangely unreal to me.

I had come for neither sea nor sunshine, but somehow to prove to my mother that all her 'dear Will' did might not be at its face value: to prevent, or at least delay indefinitely, her rush into a marriage I was sure, so very sure, would spell only disaster.

'Don't you think you might be imagining it all?' my younger sister

Nina had asked yet again this morning when we parted at our front gate, I to tote the unaccustomed luggage to my usual London-bound train, she to cycle to her job at a local children's nursery. 'But never mind, Mum will love having you there! And maybe you need a holiday, you've been — overworking — just a little?'

'Overworking' was her kind way of explaining away my fantastic suspicions. And Alan, my dear, dependable, thoughtful Alan, closest of friends, far more than friend, had an equally kind excuse: 'Ruth, exactly *how* many far-fetched crime novels have you read lately?'

It was true that beautifully-mannered, polished scoundrels set on charming gullible ladies of a certain age out of their valuables were ten a penny on paper. But it could happen too in real life! If it involved the so trustful mother I had tried to watch over since my father died, could I stand passively by?

Really the whole thing began last

year, on the day a solicitor's letter arrived announcing that our almost unknown Aunt Charlie had died (she was Mrs. Charlotte Murrell, a distant connection of Dad's) and her will named Cecily Stafford as almost sole beneficiary. I had met Aunt Charlie just once, when she came over from her French home for Dad's funeral: she was rather a family joke, a sharp-tongued eccentric lady who wore strange hats and painted even stranger pictures, who in her late sixties confounded everyone by marrying a prosperous Somebody in international banking. She outlived him by only a few years. Most of her money — along with a large, neglected house near the Sussex coast, intended possibly for his retirement — had been his.

But because Aunt Charlie had fallen out with all her relations except my transparently sincere mother, all this largesse was showered on Cecily Stafford's awed head. It was a blessing not undivided. Though her health sometimes worried us, she had been happy enough in our modest South London home, ever devoted to Nina and me, helping with a local charity, hovering busily between her circle of friends and her adored small garden.

No, the legacy hadn't helped so much. Not when the excitement made her health more frail: not when it led her to take a 'recuperating holiday' in a West Country hotel — where there happened to be staying too this man she called so reverently 'dear Will'. So very soon there was talk of her becoming Mrs. Willard Enderby. And so very soon, I believed he was already beginning to manipulate her newfound fortune!

For it was on Mr. Enderby's advice that she intended selling our home, and Aunt Charlie's decrepit country mansion was getting an extensive make-over. It was ridiculously large and unsuitable to live in, I kept insisting. And meantime, he had arranged this second stay by the sea, a prolonged one this time. 'To put the roses back in her cheeks,' he told us when he arrived to drive her to Sea Winds — but more likely, I thought grimly, to remove her from the influence of friends and family. Especially from my own suspicious eyes!

It was fortunate that Mr. Harding had a vacation lined up, so didn't object too strongly when his secretary/PA juggled the office list to fix three immediate weeks of leave. Even if he had objected, there were other jobs. My mother came first.

And if Mr. Willard Enderby objected, if my presence here would annoy him more than somewhat, at least I had achieved something!

'Is dear W — ' I started to ask, and coughed and tried again. 'Is Willard getting back tonight?'

'Oh yes. He's never away longer than he absolutely has to be. But I fill up the time,' my mother rattled on. 'Sunning in deckchairs — eating far too much, I must have put on pounds! — and there are some nice people, the Clarksons with the son in Australia — and old

Mrs. Pike, she had the same operation as poor Aunt Annie . . . oh, and that young foreign-looking lad who arrived yesterday all on his own . . . '

She made friends always with endearing ease. She chatted incautiously to people she had known minutes as though she had known them years.

But something else was on her mind than this routine gossip. All at once she bubbled over, 'Oh, Ruthie — this was meant to be a surprise for later, but I'll have to tell you now! We've fixed our wedding date!'

I just looked at her. A cloud had shadowed the evening sun.

'Seven weeks! I'll have a suit made, pale blue I thought? — all *very* quiet — and dear Will is arranging the business side, you know I'm hopeless at that! His solicitor is drawing up all the papers — '

This time I stopped her very sharply. 'All what papers?'

'Well, of course you know we're having The Old Lodge repaired and modernised —'

'To live in. Yes, and I still think it's unwise, Mum! Apart from all it's costing, why do you want the bother of a place like that?'

'But I shan't have any bother! That's what the solicitor is arranging. That's why we're putting the house in Will's name as well as mine.'

I repeated like a being entranced, 'The house. In his name.'

'So I can just enjoy it, the garden and the countryside, and get really well and strong — and look even younger than I do now, he says, he's such a flatterer! . . . '

To that I answered nothing at all. I loved her so much, in her honesty she thought was shared by everyone else. I wanted to shake her. I wanted to weep for her.

For the rest of the drive I sat in silence, hardly hearing what she said. Quite a long drive it was, and a pretty one: a steep wooded road descended a cleft in the chalky cliffs, beyond the main town, to a stretch of paved promenade along the Lower Beach, clustered with hotels. Sea Winds, one of the smallest, was white-walled and balconied, its windows commanding the expanse of the Bay, its terraced gardens set against a backdrop of green-tufted cliffs. At present I could appreciate none of it.

'Remember the boarding-house where we used to stay when you were little?' my mother was chattering on. 'All those draughts, and she always burnt the toast? — but we did have fun there! . . . Oh, is that Will's car back nice and early?'

I had spotted already the silver-grey vehicle in the hotel car-park. It should have prepared me for a tall, upright figure, equally silver-grey, equally immaculate in a dark city suit, coming quietly to meet us.

But I wasn't prepared. Angry and shaken, I struggled for a cool assurance to match his own. Already my mother was beside him, lifting a flushed cheek for his discreet salute, slipping her hand through his arm. I wanted just to bundle her back in the taxi — to drive far, far away and never look back.

'So sorry I couldn't be back in time to meet you, Ruth,' he was apologising. You would have supposed him perhaps the chair of some board, a company executive, something senior in banking: the impression of authority and experience enhanced by those very shrewd eyes — were they grey or blue? — that lighted a lean, straight-featured face surprisingly youthful, in contrast to well-smoothed silver hair. There was no arrogance in his bearing, even no obvious charm. The charisma of the man went deeper than that.

Almost I flinched away from his proffered hand. I stood there awkwardly while he insisted on paying the driver. I could pay for my own taxis!

'Will,' my mother fluttered, 'don't be cross, but — I've told her about the wedding! I couldn't wait till we can ask Nina down too and announce it then — '

'I really didn't think you'd wait,' he smiled down at her indulgently. 'Never mind, we've no secrets from Ruth, have we?'

To voice any sort of congratulations would have choked me. I wondered if either of them knew how it hurt me to see them together. The weight of my responsibility all at once was horrifying.

'Shall we go inside and get you settled in, Ruth?' he suggested pleasantly. 'You look tired, my dear. You'll find this is just the place for a nice long rest.'

★　★　★

I said, 'Alan? — Hi! Sorry to ring you so late.'

'I was hoping you'd ring,' his familiar voice reassured me across the miles. 'Are you getting settled in there?'

It was almost eleven. Out in the cool, dim garden, strings of fairy-lights circled a group of trees, here and there the flowerbeds were illuminated. All of

13

it was still unreal to me. But if 'settling down' meant shedding my formal City gear and discovering the Sea Winds admirable cuisine — and the following interlude at a terrace table with the Clarksons' Australian photos and old Mrs. Pike's surgical memoirs — then perhaps I was.

'It's nice here,' I had to admit. 'No ballrooms or banquet-halls! — but nice.' I dismissed quickly that unimportant topic. 'I need some advice. I want to know what you think.'

Last night he and Nina had teased me, offering to post on a deer-stalker cap and a magnifying glass. But now, surely, he would be convinced! If his unimaginative accountant's mind didn't fire with urgency now, it never would.

I began pouring out the frightening thing I had just learnt about The Old Lodge — that would be, after its make-over, worth a small fortune: and if Mr. Enderby chose to override any objections from my mother and put the place on the market, then promptly decamp with the proceeds, she would be robbed alike of her self-respect and her property. Alan stopped me in full tide.

'Can anyone there overhear you?'

Nobody was near the rustic bench where I was sitting with my mobile. I wouldn't have cared if they were. I went on, 'There's a wedding date fixed too — to allay suspicions, of course, when for all we know the man has a wife already! — '

He stopped me short again. 'Have you one iota of real proof for all this?'

'I knew you'd say that! I don't know how you can be so blind!'

'There's a difference between being 'blind' and jumping to conclusions. Don't you realise the trouble you might cause? Look,' he pointed out patiently, 'you dislike Mr. Enderby — all right, that's your privilege. You think your mother is making a mistake — and I agree she needs more time to consider. But does that really turn him into some sort of criminal?'

In a moment would follow his well-worn hints that a worm of jealousy might be gnawing away at me, because I wanted no stepfather invading my close-knit family.

'As for the house,' he insisted, 'if it's in their joint names once they're married, would that be so strange?'

'No! But who said anything about waiting till they're married?'

He countered, inevitably, 'Who said anything about *not* waiting?'

I bit my lip in silence. It was true I had jumped to the worst possible conclusions. Perhaps — because I had wanted to do that?

'Exactly,' he summed up. 'I'm really sorry you're so upset. But if you want my advice, do make quite sure of your facts. Solid facts, not fancies!'

I sighed rather hopelessly. The voice of sweet reason did little for me.

I pictured him in his familiar home, his kind blue eyes concerned, the lamplight on his fair hair. Of all men, he was the gentlest, the most dependable

— and the most cautious, sometimes almost maddeningly so.

I had known him now for some while. A few years older than myself, he had once been married, to the girl whose photograph in his house had always fresh flowers beside it: who died one foggy December day, her arms full of shopping, her heart full of the joy of their child's first Christmas. She was another tragic statistic in the toll of the streets.

When I first met Alan Blakely, he was still stupefied by her loss, unable to reweave the parted threads of his life. For a short while after I began my job in London at the large City Estates Company, I worked for him in Accounts — privately doctoring his letters, retrieving his mislaid files and print-outs. After I moved up to Mr. Harding, our strangely wordless friendship grew deeper. We shared library books. We spent lunchtimes with companionable packs of sandwiches, watching the grey tide of the Thames slide past.

These few years later, to his little daughter — cruelly named 'Jonquil' for her mother's favourite flower — I was now the 'Auntie Ruth' always ready for weekend games in the park or drives to the shops. And to an Alan who had very slowly learned to live again, I was . . . what was I? Dear close friend, or beloved sister? As great a part of his life as he was of mine?

We both had ties, responsibilities. Always I had known it was no use to try hastening our relationship until he was ready. Only, could I be blamed for wanting just a little more? A future more tangible, perhaps a love more urgent? . . .

'Ruth?' his voice was asking. Between us, there was often contented quiet.

'I'm still here. And I'll remember what you said. Couldn't I see you?'

'I want to see you too.'

'Then come on Sunday, make a whole day of it! Be sure Joni brings her swimsuit, she'll love it here.' I had to add, 'And you can assess 'dear Will' properly, you've only ever glimpsed him before.'

I was pleased that he agreed to come. But I was no nearer to solving the problem of Mr. Enderby.

That night I dreamt, absurdly, of the gentleman in the role of a panto villain, all twirling moustaches and manic laughter. Heavy-eyed in the morning, I wasn't a good advert for Sea Winds' comforts, arriving late for breakfast in the pleasant dining-room. Its long windows slanted sunlight across white-spread tables.

My mother said in concern, 'Ruth, you look really pale! — doesn't she, Will?'

Fresh from my lurid imaginings, I looked at him and looked away. He was suggesting a drive along the coast, for me too if I chose: but before I answered, my mother went off on one of her tangents, signalling brightly across the room. I saw a hand wave back.

'Will, that's the young fellow who

arrived yesterday,' she whispered very audibly. 'He knows all about gardens, that's the work he does! And I asked about The Old Lodge, he said — it starts with 'a' — acacias? — aubrietias? — '

'Azaleas,' a low, clear voice amended. Her new friend had made his way to us between the tables. 'Shall I chalk it on the wall for you, Mrs. Stafford?'

'Are you laughing at me again?' she protested. 'Just behave, I've my family here today! This is Mr. Enderby, my — my fiancé . . . Raymond Stenning, Will, from the 'Two Trees Nurseries' . . . Oh, and this is my Ruthie, Ray dear, I told you all about her! . . . '

I wondered what the 'all' had covered. That familiar 'Ray dear' to a day-old acquaintance hardly surprised me.

'Next time we visit the house Ray will come too, to help us with the gardens, Will,' she was explaining. 'Those shrubberies and rockeries you want — and the water-feature with a gorgeous fountain! — '

I might have guessed his plans wouldn't stop at turning the grounds into an elaborate Botanical Gardens. But it hadn't occurred to me. I choked on a protest and a toast crust, and had to drown both in coffee.

No-one seemed to notice. Willard was extending a hand and a cordial invitation, 'Yes, indeed, Mr. Stenning, I'd welcome some expert advice.'

'Oh dear me, call him 'Ray',' my mother chided. 'If Ruth's finished, why don't we all talk about it outside?'

That led to a general exodus. I followed on, to one of the seats by the lawn, to watch and listen — and ponder how, later and in privacy, I could ask a total stranger to forego a very nice commission from the Nurseries by refusing outright a large contract for The Old Lodge.

I watched him as he balanced casually on the low wall, gesturing often with very mobile hands: a man younger than I first thought, with black hair thick and straight swept off a youthfully smooth forehead, a face very alert and intelligent, most noticeable for its twin, deeply defined indentations — in a child, you would call them adorable, mischievous dimples — that lent an appealing innocence, a quick humour. A clever face, this, a face of contrasts hard to assess. Irrelevantly I compared it with Alan's, open and kind.

But there was something else about this stranger, which it seemed hadn't escaped Willard too. Either Raymond Stenning was a most inexpert expert, or he was hiding his knowledge under a bushel. Willard's queries on soil types or plant species scarcely received one specific answer. Even odder was a confusion about the site of his 'Two Trees Nurseries' in Kent — for Willard knew the area, querying 'North or South of the Sheppey Road?' Then, those over-demonstrative hands spread in a vague gesture — and left it at that.

It was my mother's plea for ruby-red roses — 'like those!', she waved towards a flowerbed — that brought a climax. 'Moonset', she was told they were. Willard asked cuttingly, 'Surely that's a white variety? Not that I'd presume to teach you your trade, Mr. Stenning. And if you'll all excuse me, I've some work to do.'

My mother went with him. I didn't follow. I watched them both back to the house, the gold-haired five-feet-one of her, the tall, well-groomed figure beside her I wished fervently worlds away.

A thought not mine alone, judging by the face Raymond Stenning made behind that retreating back. Meeting my eyes he apologised, 'Sorry! But — you can go off people! Does your Mr. Enderby always chew people up into small pieces?'

'Correction. He's not *my* Mr. Enderby!'

'Your mother's, then. Soon to be part of your family, she told me.' In his clear voice there was something that singled it out, less an accent than that purity of diction found sometimes on an alien tongue. He added, 'She also said your sister has the ravishing beauty and you the super brainpower. But surely that can't be altogether true?'

Annoyingly, I felt my colour rising. It was true, as far as the looks went: Nina took after my mother's family, the blonde, delicately attractive Cunninghams. I was, always would be, a Stafford: tall and thin, mid-brown of hair and hazel-grey of eyes like my father.

'I was so afraid Miss Stafford would turn out to be some po-faced executive type,' the teasing voice was going on. 'All power-dressing and designer specs. May I say I'm glad she didn't?'

This wasn't helping at all with the favour I needed to beg. Those very dark eyes looking into mine helped still less. I plunged before I thought better of it.

'I have to ask you something. I don't want Mum getting into any grandiose garden projects! So would you please not encourage her? I can't explain why, but it's important.'

'Not financial reasons? No, not

according to the other things she told me.'

I sighed in near despair. 'You've heard about Aunt Charlie's legacy.'

'In detail. Look, it struck me yesterday — Ruth — ' He leant a little towards me, his face all at once grave. 'Your mother is very sweet, very friendly, but she talks too much! If the wrong people heard of that big legacy . . . ? I think you should warn her to be more discreet. Or probably you already have?'

I wished Alan could hear this, Alan who thought I had overdosed on crime novels! How could it be that he understood less than this stranger? Perhaps not a stranger at all, when those disturbing eyes could look so uncannily into my mind?

He didn't smile, just the twin dimples deepening a little. He prompted, 'I'll mind my own business if you want, but I know you're worried about her. I was watching you at breakfast.'

'You were? Why were you?'

'You'll think I'm crazy if I tell you. I thought you were like your namesake — from Keats I believe, I brought down the house reciting it at a school show and I've never forgotten it. *Perhaps the selfsame song that found a path,*' the clear voice quoted, '*Through the sad heart of Ruth when, sick for home, She stood in tears amid the alien corn.* But with you it was 'cornflakes'.'

I didn't laugh. More easily, like the Ruth of those vivid lines, I could have wept. I hadn't realised till now how near to breaking down my lonely anxiety had brought me, how I had longed just for someone to share my fears.

He said softly, 'Is that your mother calling you?'

From another world I heard her cheerful summons, 'Yoo-hoo, dear! — we're leaving in the car in ten minutes, if you're coming?'

I didn't want to go, if it meant breaking this moment of warm understanding. I stood up slowly.

'Ruth,' the nearer voice asked, 'could I see you this evening? Could we go out, just the two of us? I know it's a bit sudden, but — I feel I've known you a long time.'

I could have agreed, I with all my inborn reserve, 'And I you!'

I didn't give a promise for this evening. I didn't need to. On my way back across the garden, in some fantastic way there seemed no ground beneath my feet.

* * *

Several hours went by touring in Willard's big car. Old Mrs. Pike, stout and gossipy, made up a foursome, which prevented any conversation too personal. We stopped somewhere for lunch. We surfeited on the old lady's gruesome hospital memoirs.

After that, while my mother rested, I tried in vain to ring Nina. Finally I scribbled a long letter to her up in my room. Downstairs again, I was surprised to be asked, 'Could we have a private word? — just to clear the air, Ruth?'

It was just before dinner. My mother was talking to someone out on the lawn. Willard was sitting in the lounge, and smiled at me pleasantly, indicating a chair beside his.

'Let's be blunt! I feel you're not happy about the wedding plans — or about me! Isn't that why you're here?'

I could only stare at him, confounded by this direct approach. But he seemed to expect no response. We both knew the answer. This far, we agreed.

'Can I say, your concern does you credit?' the composed voice went on. 'I know you've held the reins in your family since your father died, you feel responsible for seeing poor Cecily doesn't make a mistake. I want to assure you how much I have her interests at heart. I'll answer any questions you care to ask me.'

'Then will you please explain about the house? Where her interests come into that?'

'But surely you can see the old place would be a beautiful home. So good for her health, between the sea and the Downs! I want her to enjoy a little luxury, is there anything wrong with that?'

He hadn't mentioned what was mainly wrong, that it would not be solely her property, no longer to do with as she wished. He said smoothly, 'You're a sensible and caring young lady, but I wouldn't want that admirable sense of responsibility to run away with you. I believe you were very close to your father?'

'I was.'

'Believe me, I'm not seeking to take his place. But I do feel I can make Cecily happy. She's very special to me. So can't we be friends, my dear?'

I looked at him, and I could only wonder, how did you penetrate a mind so unfathomable? He was insisting, 'That's what your mother wants. So it's up to us, isn't it?'

I saw her then, standing in the

doorway, beaming with pleased surprise at finding us together. The contest of wits would have to wait a while.

I sat baffled and mainly silent through dinner. We were almost finished when my mother had another cause for surprise: she repeated after me in disbelief, 'You've a *date* — with Ray Stenning? Whatever would your Alan say, Ruthie?'

I tried to say there was no law against spending an evening with someone else. But she was drifting on, 'Mind you, I'm not surprised he asked you. He's got what it takes, I daresay he's quite a young scamp!' She peered across at his table, but I had purposely waited till it was empty. 'It's really quite romantic! You know, he's not exactly good-looking — but those eyes, they must be Italian or Spanish . . . wouldn't you say he has some Mediterranean blood? . . . '

Unexpectedly, Willard broke in, 'Before you ladies get too carried away, is this really a good idea? We know next to nothing about young Stenning. He certainly didn't impress me too favourably this morning.'

I said stiffly, 'I'm not a schoolgirl.' My mother was protesting too, quite indignantly, 'Will, I got to know him really well yesterday! He must be lonely here all by himself — he hasn't any close family — and *such* charming manners! . . . '

She was always loyal to her friends. She was still protesting when I slipped away into the garden.

A sprinkler was playing on the grass. The scent of those nameless roses was sweet in the evening air. I found him waiting on the same low wall.

He said simply, 'You didn't forget?'

Had he really thought I might? I shook my head.

The face that had haunted me all day was quiet and questioning. 'But you've not had a good day, I can see. Maybe some music at the Floral Arcade might help?'

As we walked to the car-park, I was conscious of his lesser height than

Alan's beside me. I was aware too this was sober, feet-on-the-ground Miss Stafford's first time of going out, for year upon long year, with anyone but Alan. I wondered, when would I wake up?

As well came another fleeting thought. Had any man the right to a smile quite like this?

2

'Sorry about the transport. Especially as it's standing next to the old boy's limo,' my escort apologised.

The car being opened up for me was certainly a contrast to that gleaming silver-grey job. I scrambled into a tatty green soft-top, obviously advanced in years and mileage. But what it lacked in looks it made up in noisy power. I clung to my seat as we roared uphill.

'Forgive the muddle in here,' he was apologising again. 'I've been a bit busy.'

Littered around us were papers and notebooks, spilling from a briefcase lettered 'R.S.' There were a few issues of *The Gardener* and *Horticulture Monthly*. I said unkindly, 'Were you swotting up on roses?'

'That's not nice, Miss Stafford. I did wonder if old Enderby would advise you against coming out with me. Did he?'

More and more he must be a mind reader. I agreed, 'He did!'

'He's a bit too sharp. It took him just minutes to label me a fool or a phoney. Don't tell me you didn't notice.' He was frowning at the road ahead. 'He can think what he likes, but — what did you think?'

'If it helps, I'm sure you're very far from a fool!'

'Which makes me a phoney. Right.' He muttered something I didn't catch, except I realised that if he chose to swear he had the grace to use another language.

We were halfway up that picturesque hill winding from the Lower Beach, at a gravelled 'viewing point' commanding a shimmering seascape. All at once he turned the car in sharply. It scrunched to a halt.

'Look,' I said uneasily, 'I thought we were going to — '

'We still are. But you're too honest to

talk to in riddles all evening, I think I must come clean before we get started. I'll trust you not to give me away.'

Before I could question that last ominous phrase, he was opening the dashboard cupboard in front of me. I stared at assorted recorders and cameras — and several printed introduction cards. Some were inscribed, *Raymond Stenning, Two Trees Nurseries*, but only some. I gazed blankly at a handful of other identities.

'Tools of the trade,' he explained. 'No-one notices 'Richard Strange, Antiques', or 'Robert Steyner, Photographer' — or usually not our ignorant friend 'R. Stenning, Horticulturalist', which I'm using this time. But if I booked into the hotel as Raoul Renato Stevenson, Enquiry Agent — or 'private eye', if you like — the person I'm shadowing would vanish like a scalded cat . . . you do see that? . . . '

For a moment I sat there in silence. I stammered at last, 'Then you — you're really — ?'

'A private detective. Yes, there are

such people! — doing quite sordid routine jobs, none of the glamour films and television give us! But for me it's just a fill-in until I can get back to the stage, that's my first and last love.'

'I see. I think I can imagine that. The real professional stage?'

'Yes, indeed. Abroad, you wouldn't have heard of me.'

I nodded, gradually beginning to absorb this startling story. 'And what did you say your real name is?'

'Stevenson comes from a sober, solid British father. The rest from my mother, who was an actress, part French and part Italian. The likeness shows, don't tell me!'

'It does,' I agreed. 'Mum warned me you must have Latin Blood and I must Beware!'

The hands he spread extravagantly in protest were a give-away in themselves.

'I've lived all around everywhere — but I was at school quite a while in London. You can't say my English isn't superb?'

I agreed again, 'It's fantastic!' and smiled to myself as I listened to the rest of the story. Not that it was a very happy tale: his father had died when he was a child, his mother more lately, leaving him with just a few relatives dotted around Europe. The majority of his twenty-four years (amazingly, he was several years my junior — in time if certainly not in experience) had been spent across the Channel. 'Drifting,' he freely confessed.

'But now you have this job, and you're investigating someone at Sea Winds,' I said, quite matter-of-fact now — until a sudden idea hurled me back on my own troubles. 'Not Mr. Enderby?'

'No, not him.' He asked quietly, 'Why, do you think he needs investigating?'

The shock of the idea had turned me ice-cold. I was aware all at once of two hands holding both mine, warming and steadying.

'Forgive me, I've made you upset. Won't you let me help? — I'm trusting you with all my secrets, so can't you trust me too? I've seen you watching this Enderby guy ... don't look so startled, it's my job to notice things ...'

I denied nothing, clinging fast now to those comforting hands. He prompted, 'We've never really been strangers, have we? Isn't that why we're here now?'

That, too, I didn't deny. But however much my ordinary, organised world was wobbling on its axis, surely for my dear mother's sake this was a heaven-sent opportunity?

Nor did my inborn caution, second only to Alan's, raise any objections. If my mother would be angry and horrified, that was a price to be paid. If Alan might never understand, that too I must risk. Indeed, with these persuasive hands on mine so melting my senses, could I think clearly of Alan at all?

The decision had to be made, and I made it.

'You're right, I'm afraid I do need help. For my mother — er — Raoul? —'

I had two tries at pronouncing the un-familiar name.

'Settle for 'Steve' if you like, my friends often find it easier. What can I do?' he said simply.

'I'll tell you. I'm not on holiday any more than you are, but I just don't know where to start. I need to find out everything about Mr. Enderby, his business, his background — whether he's really the model of respectability he looks! Because — I suspect he's trying to trick Mum out of her money, let alone break her heart in a very loathsome way. Is that the sort of thing you could deal with?'

There was no sceptical amusement in the dark, clever face that had screwed a little almost as though with pain. He said, 'Yes, it does sound loathsome. But it's very much the sort of thing I deal with.'

'Good! Only I must warn you, it's all really intuition. I know this is a very serious accusation to make, and I haven't one atom of real proof.'

I had to explain that, the same confession Alan always drew from me. But there the similarity ended.

'No, you wouldn't have any, if the man knows what he's doing. Never mind, if there's a way to beat him at his nasty little game, we'll find it, I promise.'

I gazed at him almost in disbelief. It seemed such an age that I had been trying to scale this precipice alone.

'We'll find it,' the reassuring voice said again. 'We'll do it together. We'll make a good partnership — yes?'

Another car was drawing in beside us, its radio blaring. The peace of our confiding and understanding was shattered. My hands were dropped with one last pressure, the noisy engine started up.

'We can still make the Arcade,' Steve said. 'It's a nice music show, so I've been told. You like music, Ruth? — and afterwards we'll get started, you can tell me all the details. Soon Mr. Enderby won't know what's hit him!'

I wondered, as the dusty green car roared on up the hill, would I ever know exactly what had hit *me*?

★ ★ ★

Sunday morning, the morning after the night before, dawned wholly beautiful. It would blossom into a warm, sunlit day. The best summer for a decade, all the weather-pundits were cooing.

I took extra trouble after showering to add a dash of hitherto unused 'Secret Rhapsody' perfume that Mum gave me on a recent birthday. I brushed out my long hair, and in place of the usual formal knot arranged a bobbing pony-tail. I took more trouble choosing a scoop-neck top and a flowery, floaty skirt.

After all, this was the seaside, it was high summer! I was a world away from Mr. Harding's dreary E-mails and reports and travel bookings. And wasn't Alan visiting today?

He was even here already, parking in

his slow and careful way.

'Auntie Ruth,' Jonquil's excited voice greeted me, 'I've brought my swimsuit like you said, the new pink one! We got up ever so early to get here! — '

It was still not ten o'clock. People were dawdling and chatting round the hotel and the gardens after breakfast. Mrs. Pike was knitting something unidentifiable on the pleasant terrace and monitoring us over her glasses.

'It's ever so nice here!' The child was gazing round large-eyed. 'I wish we didn't have to go home again. Daddy, could I miss school just one little day? . . . '

Over her enraptured head I met the quiet smile of Alan's blue eyes, always comfortable and comforting. Today, a little less so. I asked him unoriginally, 'Did you have a good journey? What a good idea to bring Nina along too!'

My sister was just emerging from the car. I always thought she looked like our mother would have done years ago, when Cecily Cunningham broke hearts by the score — as she still enjoyed telling us. Today Nina was in fragile white (being one of those lucky mortals able to stay unsoiled by long journeys) with her pale-gold hair falling loose in all its glory.

'Lovely to see you, Nina. You look a picture,' I said, and meant it. 'Mum will be so pleased you're here — '

I got no further, for already an excited voice was exclaiming, 'Joni, you've grown another inch! — Alan, how are you, dear? — Nina, what a lovely surprise! — '

Willard was beside her, ready with outstretched hand to welcome the visitors. He stooped to Jonquil's height to smile her out of sudden shyness. Always he had the right word at the right moment, you had to grant him that.

Alan as usual made heavy weather of small talk, hanging back when the others drifted inside. I lingered too by the colourful flowerbeds.

'I wouldn't say no to a few weeks

here.' He glanced around admiringly. 'Ruth, are you any happier yet, about your mother?'

'Not much. But I've started my campaign moving!'

'You have?' Concern creased lines into his forehead, sobering still more the fair, thoughtful face I knew so well. 'But didn't we agree, first make quite sure of the facts?'

It didn't help that we were sitting on that low wall where Steve waited for me last night. Last night that held me still in a dream, that made it hard to talk normally today to anyone at all — and to Alan, almost impossible.

Would I ever forget that long, long evening, starting with its shocks and decisions, ending with sheer enchantment? The music that set racing even the prosaic blood of Ruth Stafford, the Floral Arcade turned into a fantasy of glass looking out to dusky sky and arcs of fairy-lights — and most of all the time after by the late evening shore, the hand of a stranger holding mine, the smile, the nearness of him. And then the drive back, the moment of farewell on the moonlit hotel lawn, black eloquent eyes that seemed to look into my very soul, caressing lips gently touching mine . . . which moved my mother, unashamedly peeking from her window, to rhapsodise mistily, 'Ruthie, dear, so *romantic*! . . .'

That was yesterday. This was today, when I must explain to my so devoted, dependable Alan how I had ignored all his sane advice, I had even enlisted the aid of a professional sleuth — though not professional enough to refrain from kissing a new client in the moon-light? . . .

It must be said, at least most of it. Though it meant breaking a solemn promise in revealing the truth about 'Raymond Stenning', Alan could be trusted implicitly.

He repeated, 'Raoul Renato Steven-son. Quite sure it wasn't Wolfgang Smith? Or Diego Brown?'

I explained uneasily, 'You see, he

trusted me with his real identity, he offered to give up his time to help sort out Willard. So for Mum's sake, how could I refuse? I knew you'd be cross, but — '

'It's not for me to be cross. I just wish you'd made sure this man is genuine first of all.'

'What's that supposed to mean?' I was spurred to ask sharply.

'Isn't it fairly obvious? If Mr. Stenning, Gardener, is a plausible disguise, couldn't Mr. Stevenson, Investigator, be another?' With rare vehemence, Alan thrust out an emphasising hand. 'There's something odd about this, it's all too convenient! You tell a perfect stranger you're on a detective mission — and hey presto, it turns out he's a detective himself, eager to take over from you!'

'It's just a coincidence Steve's here on a case,' I defended.

He let pass the familiar 'Steve'. 'He told you that, but does that make it true? What sort of case?'

'He couldn't say because it's confidential. And quite right too!'

'I hope he's not charging you a big fee?'

'He wouldn't hear of a fee! I did offer to pay for his time, but — '

I stopped short there. It was the height of irony that every effort to make Alan distrust Willard Enderby was unavailing — but he dreamed up instantly these suspicions about Steve! Just because Steve was legitimately using an assumed name! Or perhaps because Alan was human, and Alan was *jealous* . . . ?

We had never quarrelled, we two. At any other moment I would be remorseful for hurting him: but now I began quite angrily, 'Will you just try to understand? — '

The question stayed unfinished. I tailed off into an urgent whisper, 'We'll discuss it later!'

Steve was strolling along the path to us. The thought of this meeting had been worrying me. Now, seeing together these two so dissimilar men emphasised the tall, undemonstrative presence of

Alan, a little staid, always — until today — so kind: I looked from his face to another, youthful and alert, indented by just a glimmer of innocent dimples.

I hadn't seen Steve since last night, missing him at breakfast. I found myself fluttering in a way worthy of my mother, 'Oh, Steve — no, you're not intruding! — I wanted you to meet Alan ... ' Understanding his quick warning look I added, 'Yes, I did explain the names, but Alan won't tell a soul.'

I felt my face burning. Last night was all at once so near. I watched a formal hand-shake accompanying Alan's invariably polite words.

'It's kind of you to help Ruth. But I'm afraid you'll just waste your time.'

'Could any time spent helping Ruth be wasted?'

'Oh. Well.' Alan coughed, sticking to his ground. 'My guess is, too much far-fetched crime fiction.'

'Maybe, maybe not,' Steve said gravely.

It was a relief to see Joni running towards us, bubbling over with the news that we were all taking a picnic lunch down to the beach.

Whether anyone invited Steve to be part of that 'all' I never knew. But when we set off soon after, he was there. Willard possibly, Alan certainly, might have objected: but Alan always avoided arguments, and Mr. Enderby merely raised an expressive eyebrow.

No-one else minded. Not Mum, chattering in her shaded chair, enjoying equally the midsummer shore and the Stenning/Stevenson smile. Not Joni nor Nina, both timid with strangers but accepting readily this particular stranger so good at impromptu beach games — who bowled an outraged Mr. Enderby out first ball in a makeshift game of cricket. ('I wasn't ready, boy,' he took pains to point out.)

Presently Nina and I began sorting out the lavish hotel lunch basket. Steve, 'to cool off,' he said, ran down to the water and struck out strongly far into the Bay, till his dark head was a dot in the sparkle of water and my mother fretted, 'Will, can he get back all that way?' Willard, glancing over his newspaper, drily reassured her, 'I'm sure he knows what he's doing.'

He was right. Steve arrived back safely, to be scolded by my mother, plied hesitantly with coffee by Nina, hailed by an admiring Jonquil, 'That was great, Mr. Stenning! In the baths I always sink to the bottom, even when Daddy's holding me!'

Steve smiled at the eager child, long-legged in her bright pink swimsuit. 'Too bad. How about a lesson from me?'

'Would you really? Daddy,' she shrilled, 'can I? — please? — '

Alan was plainly seeking a reason to refuse, and couldn't find one. As Joni pranced to the water's edge, Willard said, 'A man of many talents, Cecily, your young protégé — except when it involves gardening. But I really can't understand what you and Ruth see in him.'

'Can't you, Will dear?' my mother murmured demurely. Her little smile implied that no woman between six and ninety-six would be so baffled.

A short while later Joni returned to us, string-haired and ecstatic. Clinging to Steve's hand across a patch of pebbles, she bawled from yards away, 'I swam! — all by myself! — well, six strokes, I've never ever done six before!'

'It was just her timing needed putting right, Alan,' Steve explained.

Alan's answer, as he towelled his daughter's hair, was inaudible.

A little apart from the others, beside my deck-chair, Steve collapsed prone on the sand to dry off. And it was then that last night and today became one. I sat still just watching him, how sun and water were adding a pleasing depth to the bronze of his skin, how the black drenched hair fell over his forehead, and that alert face was so appealing and innocent in repose.

I was still the Ruth Stafford supposed to possess more brains than beauty. My head should be screwed on no less firmly for one fairytale outing, or this glory of summer and a stranger's presence near me. But I knew the nameless excitement I felt was something I had never known before. Not ever with Alan, my constant companion for so long, whose life was to be my life . . .

'Now come along, people, who's ready for lunch?' my mother was asking.

* * *

It was a long day, the kind to cherish in memory, even though Steve and I were never once alone. When finally we all left the beach, he murmured an excuse and vanished. I devoted myself to the guests, doing my best to avoid any private moments with Alan.

But he cornered me himself, in the almost deserted hotel lounge. I gazed at him unhappily. I thought he looked weary and worried.

'Ruth, I came here to try to help you. We don't seem to have got very far.'

'No,' I muttered. 'But you can still help me a lot! You've seen plenty of 'dear Will' now close up. What do you make of him?'

His guarded answer was all I expected. 'I can't really judge from a few hours on the beach. But I've seen nothing remotely suspicious about the man.'

I heaved a resigned sigh. However, he had more to say.

'But I've an idea that might help. Anyway, it can't do any harm. You remember Robert Collyer, who was in the Legal Section at the office, and then went into private practice? — I've known him for years, we're good friends. Suppose he were asked to supervise your mother's financial interests, and we told him the whole situation in confidence. Would that ease your mind?'

'It might,' I conceded. 'Only, shouldn't we consult Steve first?'

I couldn't remember when Alan's mild eyes opened so wide. He exclaimed, 'Why in heaven's name should we do that?'

'He's taking over the investigation, so he has to know! Will you wait while I find him?'

There was no need to look far, for a glance from the window showed Jonquil monopolising her new idol in the garden. I tapped on the glass, and he came in at once.

As I explained Alan's idea, it brought to Steve's face a rare frown.

'Well, I don't know. You're sure this guy is reliable, Alan?'

'I've known 'this guy' several years.' (Clearly Alan implied, 'Far longer than any of us have known you!') 'Robert is highly competent. Mrs. Stafford surely won't take it amiss if I suggest putting a new client my friend's way.'

'No, she mightn't. But old Enderby might! — or hasn't that struck you? I believe he's having her legal affairs dealt with along with his own. If you suddenly insist on a change, won't it put him on his guard at once?'

'Which will make it even harder to nail him,' I had to agree. 'Yes, that's good sense!'

Indeed, it was: little as I wanted to oppose Alan, or especially to side with Steve against him. I hoped very much Alan wouldn't argue.

And he didn't, typically avoiding anything like a scene. But before leaving he found another moment alone with me, to thank me with quiet, strained hurt for inviting him here for the day: 'At least Nina and Joni enjoyed it, so I suppose it wasn't a total waste of time and petrol.'

He didn't go in for sarcasm, as a rule. But nor, as a rule, did I beg his advice and then fly in the face of it — let alone dally with more blatantly attractive men under his nose. If he wanted me to feel guilty, he was succeeding.

And yet, there flared an answering spark of resentment. Had he any right to take this injured tone? It wasn't my fault that our relationship had never become still closer, that never had he asked me to be his wife! Many times I had expected it to happen. Many times the vacuum of emptiness in my busy life had yawned a little wider.

So Alan Blakely, to whom I had given years of companionship and sympathy, needn't behave like a martyr! I had just acted for the best as I saw it. Rather frostily I asked, 'Aren't you being a bit childish about all this? You don't have to throw your toys out of the pram, do you?'

Even those mildest of eyes could light with anger. He said, 'If we're descending to insults, it's time I went home.'

And he went, hustling his passengers into the car, ignoring Joni's plaintive protests. Among all the waving hands and farewells I stood angrily, miserably, not far from tears.

Later that evening, when this first ever real quarrel between us seemed suddenly so foolish, I almost rang him. But I didn't ring.

In the morning I was tempted again to call him. I didn't do it then either.

He could ring me, had he anything new to say. Or if he hadn't what use was there in aggravating wounds still too fresh to be healed?

3

From Whitedene's Esplanade, coaches ran daily to view Southampton's shipping, or inland around the Southern countryside. Speedboats creamed white foam across the Bay, bigger boats explored the coastline. Shops and shows, breezy cliff walks, offered a change from the beach. Steve and I tried them all.

On other holidays over the years I had visited the misted crags and castles of Scotland, I had seen Paris and Vienna, as well as several pleasant breaks with Alan and Joni staying with his grandparents in Devon. At present I wasn't really supposed to be on holiday at all. But I had never known days like these, never before this magic that was reborn each new morning with the smile in a man's dark eyes.

I knew it was Steve who lent the sun its extra radiance and the sea its wondrous azure. Often, I couldn't believe this was happening. Sometimes too there was a sharp stab of unease — because still I hadn't patched up my quarrel with Alan.

But when I was with Steve that disturbing thought came scarcely ever. And I was with him so much. The 'case' that first brought him here, he told me, had petered out: 'But that's given me more time for you! — and if they want me back in London they'll have to come and fetch me.'

His usual half-serious approach to duty, maybe. And his attentions to me were probably usual as well, for I couldn't imagine I was the first to succumb to this spell. But I didn't ask, I didn't want to know. It was enough to push aside the past and live from day to sunshine day.

Except for one shade on the horizon that couldn't be much longer ignored — as nearer drew the time my mother, my mother's property, would be committed to Willard Enderby.

'But of course,' Steve said surprisingly, 'you could be quite wrong.'

Last night we saw a play, and afterwards lingered in a sandwich bar while he entertained me with criticisms of the performance. He even re-enacted some of the parts with uncanny accuracy, and I realised how much he really did know about the stage. This morning we had set out along the cliffs, and now were dawdling back. I sat on the rough grass watching streaks of white cloud above the Bay.

Over breakfast Willard had been scanning two letters, one from his lawyer, one from the builders renovating The Old Lodge. That had jolted me into a guilty panic at the precious time I had wasted — or Steve and I had wasted together.

But . . . 'You could be wrong,' he said now again. 'I haven't told you, but I've been contacting some sources. And old Enderby really is in legitimate business as an Investment Consultant. No black marks to his name.'

He was lying on the grass beside me, his face upturned to mine unusually earnest. I countered, 'Does it follow he's being legitimate with Mum?'

'No. But it seems unlikely he'd take risks with his reputation.'

'Or risk landing himself in jail!' I said bluntly. 'If he's a cruel, money-grabbing rogue, the sooner he gets his come-uppance the better, so innocent folk can sleep safely in their beds. Those sorts of frauds and tricksters deserve to be behind bars for a long, long time!'

To that Steve answered a slightly uncertain 'Oh!' His face puckered a little wryly, maybe in surprise at my vehemence. But he had more arguments to offer.

'You don't mind if I say this? — but couldn't you be a bit biased? You don't want an outsider in your family, so you need an excuse to stop your mother remarrying?'

I turned my head away, probably looking as disappointed as I felt. So often, by both Alan and Nina, I had been accused of jealousy! Even if it were true, did that make my mother's possible danger any the less?

'Now I've made you angry. Yes?'

'No!' I said stiffly. 'I've just heard it all before. I'm not keen on acquiring a stepfather, but most of all I don't see 'dear Will' as a man you can trust. Do you think I'd try to bust up poor Mum's marriage otherwise?'

For an instant the black eyes seemed to waver from mine, falling in a way unlike him. He muttered a subdued, 'No, ma'am.' Then again he looked up at me — and unexpectedly pulled my face down to his.

There had been other kisses and caresses in our few days together, warm and half-playful, with teasing murmurs that a 'chaste English rose' must pardon his 'desperate Continental blood'. All part of the laughter and understanding we shared, the sunshine glow all around. But now he kissed me strongly, tenderly, his lips totally possessing mine. It was the first time quite like that.

'Ruth, forgive me, I promised to help with your trouble — and I haven't helped, I've wanted only to spend this time here with you. But I'll do better now, I swear to you! — '

The barest trace of an accent had become a little stronger, the faultless English a trifle stilted, the first time I had known that too.

'I need to go to London. I'll see some people, do some asking around — maybe find more truths about Enderby. Shall I go today, catch the next train?'

'If — if you think it's best,' I said. I could have added, without him the rest of the day would be long and empty. We started straight back to the hotel, and I watched him unlock his car to run to the station.

'I might be late back. But I'll ring you,' he said. And then, 'I'll miss you.'

Again the lingering kiss blurred my senses. I clung to him with all my strength, his face against mine. For this moment, it seemed all the world stilled.

When I drifted inside soon afterwards for lunch, I feared my mother would notice something different about me, but she seemed not to. She was feeling tired today, planning a quiet afternoon on the terrace. It gave me an excuse to linger around with an unopened magazine, waiting and waiting for Steve's call.

It was almost six when my phone jangled, out in the garden. The voice that greeted me again gained an alien inflection across the dividing miles.

'Sorry to take so long. I've a big shocker for you, so hang on to your hat!'

I said foolishly, 'I haven't got a hat.'

'Then hang on to your head, you'll need to. If your Mum expected to be Mrs. Enderby number one, she's mistaken. He was married before — to a Miss Beatrice Withers, twenty years older, in poor health — who died six months after, leaving him a fair sum of money. How about that, cherie?'

At this moment the appealing word

of endearment was lost on me. For so long I was silent that he asked, 'Ruth, did you hear? I found out from some golfing crony of Willard's — by standing him more drinks than he could handle. Willard married her a few years back, a lady of mature years with a nice mature bank balance. She died after falling on some steps. If you want I'll try to find out more?'

I didn't answer that directly. I muttered, 'Mum hasn't ever breathed a word of knowing about it. Steve — what do you honestly think?'

'Maybe the lady thought her six months worth the money. Who knows? But 'dear Will' could have a better write-up as a future bridegroom.'

I would have put it far more strongly. Would a man who once married for money scruple to do it over again?

Already my first shock was fading. I blurted out, 'Well, I'll tell Mum — I'll do it right away. When she knows he has this secret up his sleeve she might have second thoughts! Only — ' I trailed off miserably, 'she's going to be very upset.'

'I'm so sorry.' There was an answering distress in his voice. 'If you wait till I get back, we could tell her together?'

It was so like him, this warmth of concern: so like the Steve I was coming to understand more each day, whose outward flamboyance overlaid a nature so deeply caring. But I said, 'I think I must tell her now. But — please hurry back.'

He promised, 'I'll hurry.'

The longer I waited, the worse my task would be. I knew my mother had gone to her room to change for dinner. I tapped on her door.

She was sitting at the dressing-table, and turned to me with a smile so unsuspecting it was like a blow.

'Is Will back yet, Ruthie? He said we could go for a drive this evening.'

'He isn't back yet. Mum — I've got to talk to you seriously.'

As I sat down on the bed she swivelled round, not yet alarmed. She suggested, 'About you and Ray, dear? — I've been wanting a little word about that. He's wonderful fun to go around with — and I always think a little holiday fling hurts no-one, I'm sure I had lots when I was a girl — and you work so hard, sometimes I think you're just too sober and sensible! — ' She paused to gulp in breath. 'But don't get too involved. Will really does think you shouldn't trust him too far.'

That was an irony to challenge all belief! But I couldn't let myself be angry.

'I came to talk about something else. Did you know — that Willard has been married before?'

I was aware of my own heartbeats, of those summer-blue eyes so vulnerable to hurt. Yet there was no real shock or pain in them, only surprise.

'Oh, how did you find that out? About poor Beatrice Withers?'

For a second time tonight I was struck dumb.

'Of course Will told me, before we

agreed to get married. She was a very old friend — a dear soul who was kind to his mother years before. He married her to care for her in her last years, when she was sick and alone. Just like dear Will to devote his life to someone in need! Only poor Beatrice didn't live very long.' She smiled at me earnestly. 'I did mean you and Nina to know sometime. But Will never speaks of it, it's such a personal thing.'

It was the first secret she had kept in her life. She asked again, quite reasonably, 'But how did you find out?'

I mumbled that Ray had met in some London club or bar an old friend of Willard's. She shook her head over Mr. Enderby's intimate affairs being discussed over too many drinks. Dear Will wouldn't like it at all. I assured her Ray wouldn't broadcast the story.

I left her to finish dressing, and soon after endured a meal that half choked me, facing an urbane Willard across our table. When they left for their drive, I haunted the hotel like a restless ghost, waiting for a dusty green car to skid into the car-park. When it did, I needed badly the arms that held me close.

'He'd told her already,' I whispered. 'At least, his version. And she thinks he did a wonderful thing looking after the woman. Oh, I'm getting so muddled — maybe he did?'

'Perhaps. Helped by the wonderful bank balance?'

'I just don't know! Steve, what am I going to do?'

If that appeal found no real answer, at least its urgency was a little eased when we found a seat by the sands, we sat quietly close together. Held in his arms, I watched the darkening sky, the evening tide swirling into dim mystery.

Today had proved one thing, just one. Whatever unkind things people said about Steve, it had proved my faith in him, my need for him — my joy in him.

Alan rang me on the Friday. At last he did, from the office at lunchtime. I imagined him doodling precise geometric patterns with the pen I gave him last Christmas. He said, 'I've been so worried about you, I made a real nonsense of the departmental balances.'

It seemed a year, not barely a week, since we were together. Flaring resentments had cooled.

I said I was sorry not to have rung him — and meant it: I was sorry too about that foolish tiff. And yes, Steve was still helping me (I explained briefly about Beatrice Withers) but the puzzle remained unsolved. And tomorrow, we were all to visit The Old Lodge to inspect the builders' progress.

Almost I was tempted to invite him along too on that visit. But it would be asking for trouble. Steve would be there — invited by my mother (she laughed off Willard's half-serious objections) to advise on the gardens.

Obviously that invitation had put Steve in a quandary. He asked me privately, 'Do I wriggle out of it, or try to bluff it through?' We chose the latter, because I so much wanted him to see the house and hear all the plans for it, to form his own assessment of Mr. Enderby's behaviour.

So Saturday afternoon found us sharing the back of Willard's opulent car. Despite the importance of the occasion, as we glided through green Sussex lanes, Steve managed enough whispers behind the gentleman's dignified back to dissolve us into muffled laughter. I saw the searching Enderby eyes monitoring us disapprovingly in the rear mirror.

'There, Ray!' My mother glowed with excitement as the car swung in at a gateway surmounted by two battered urns. 'What do you think of my little property?'

Little, it wasn't. There were heaps of builders' impedimenta about, the tatty paintwork was only partly renewed: but you had to admit, the ivy-clad walls and dark timbers of the spreading old house had style and majesty, mellow in the sunshine against a sweep of uncut grass and overgrown trees. I saw Steve's face become suddenly graver. Maybe I had disparaged the place too much with my 'old barn' descriptions. Maybe it really *was* inducement enough for Mr. Enderby to do ... whatever Mr. Enderby was doing? ...

'Just look at that awful grass! — Ray, now where would be best for my rose-garden?' my mother was asking, and then broke off, spotting another car on the weed-encroached drive. 'Oh, we've got visitors! It's Alan and Nina! Ruth, did you ask them along?'

I hadn't asked them, but I had told Alan the details. I realised anew the depth of his anxiety, enough even to bring him here so untypically 'gate-crashing'.

'It's quite like a house-warming,' my mother beamed. 'I wonder if the kitchen is done yet? — we did choose the 'Apple Blossom' colour, didn't we, Will ... ?'

I greeted Alan with an awkward mumble. I watched him nod to Steve quite politely.

As well, I didn't miss something else among the greetings: the bright-haired vision of my sister in purest daffodil, like a glory of sunlit beauty, shyly lowering her gaze as she touched Steve's outstretched hand. She coloured up at his confidential murmur, 'What wonderful dream did you walk out from?'

Well, Steve was Steve. Those melting dark eyes were born to rove a little. It was their likely effect on my impressionable sister that bothered me a little.

'What are we waiting for, everyone? — let's go in!' my mother hustled us.

Whoever built this house must have sought to alarm future residents, not only with unexpected mirrors inset in panelled walls bringing you face to face with yourself, but by hiding rooms round corners and down blind passages. An atmosphere of paint and plaster pervaded the echoing rooms with their sprinkling of furniture eerily sheeted. Yet attractive features were abundant, handsome fireplaces, a gracious curving staircase.

The work already done proved the potential of the place. It would finally be worth a small fortune. My mother's, not Mr. Enderby's!

'Mum, it'll be perfect,' Nina told her, moved beyond shy reticence among so many people. I couldn't help watching my sister — and watching Steve watching her. In one of those startling mirrors I surveyed the three of us, aware of the pair of them standing together like a cameo of youth and summertime. My hair hadn't gone right this morning. My last year's denim skirt wasn't the greatest.

Edging past Mr. Enderby, stationed in the hall like a bland, silver-haired monarch of all he beheld, I went upstairs to look around alone. Through several empty rooms I peered and poked, hoping viciously Willard would be plagued by dodgy plumbing and legions of ravenous woodworms. It was a sudden utterly chilling sound, above the footsteps and voices around the house, that jolted those thoughts from my mind.

I heard a scream. Distant but unmistakable, it was a woman's scream.

Headlong I rushed and clattered back down to ground level, and down again to the extensive cellars burrowing beneath the old house. One had been fitted up for storing wine, the others were just black, cobwebby cavities.

'Cecily, it's all right,' Willard was reassuring her, seeming to be capably in charge. 'Just take it easy, my dear.'

Evidently she had ventured down there, bent on inspecting every inch of the place — and found herself suddenly, frighteningly, shut in. I wasn't surprised at her terror. She had an equal dread of the dark, of confined spaces, and spiders. All three at once could well produce near hysteria.

But it wasn't the fitful sobs that alarmed me. Her grey face, the way she reeled on her feet, pointed to more than passing fright.

Willard lifted her in his arms to carry her gently upstairs to fresher air and blessed daylight. She clung to him weakly. The rest of us milled round, trying to help. It was Alan who uncovered for her a shrouded sofa. Nina knelt to hold her hand, the daffodil dress trailing on dusty floorboards.

'Will, I'm all right . . . but — this house is quite scary . . . one moment the main light was on, and then — everything went dark! — '

'You know the electrics down there are being replaced,' he reassured her.

'Yes, but — the door started creaking shut . . . oh, if Ray hadn't rushed in and rescued me I think I'd have died!'

'Just the draught,' Willard said patiently. 'You're not saying we've a resident ghost?'

She shook her head, but she couldn't manage a smile. 'I just want to go back to the hotel. Please, let's go back.'

He soothed her firmly, 'Now this is foolish. You need one of your tablets

— still in the car, are they?' He glanced round, his gaze falling first on Steve. 'Would you be helpful again? — they're locked up in the front.'

He tossed across his keys. Steve, startled from a frowning preoccupation, only just caught them.

Willard waited a moment more to be sure the patient was improving and then went off to the kitchen for some water, his steps echoing down the rear passageway. The big bare room suddenly was still.

My mother opened very blue eyes to murmur, 'Oh, what a nuisance I'm being.'

'Mum,' Nina whispered, 'you felt like this the time you thought we had burglars. And in that bad thunderstorm. Shouldn't you tell Dr. Harris?'

'Mum,' I asked more concisely, 'what sort of tablets are you having?'

She answered neither question directly. She gave a little sigh.

'Girls, I'm going to tell you something in confidence, I *don't* want it to go outside the family. No, don't go, Alan,' she smiled up at him, 'you're almost family! You see, Dr. Harris gave me the tablets, and Will always makes sure to bring them when we're out. They're for my heart. I had tests at the hospital, I didn't tell you. Just like silly me to get some complicated heart problem — but I'll be around for years and years if I take things quietly. Only — it's quite a serious thing, Dr. Harris says . . . '

A second secret she had kept, far more shattering than the first. Her voice went murmuring on, she hadn't wanted to alarm us, but dear Will knew all about it and he would look after her, hadn't we just seen how well? And she couldn't be ill anyway tomorrow, with his solicitor coming down specially with the draft papers for transferring the house — and her new will . . .

I held her hand tightly. I repeated, 'You're making a new will?'

Scarcely I needed to hear her jumbled explanations why it would be largely in Willard's favour: 'He'll always treat you girls as though you were his own! — but Aunt Charlie's shares and investments are best with him because he knows all about those things — you do see that? — '

I couldn't tell her all I saw. That the plan of Willard Enderby was to obtain not just this house but the rest of her legacy as well: that if she seemed likely to survive for those 'years and years', a few convenient frights like today's might so easily hasten an ending!

From the pale, unsuspecting face beside me I looked up, and across the room saw watching another face, almost as familiar as hers. And at long last, I read a shocked, stern understanding in Alan's serious eyes.

★ ★ ★

Safely back at Sea Winds, my mother wheeled like a banished child, 'Must I really go to bed already?'

But she let us persuade her up to her

pleasant room (it was marred only by the photo of Willard by the bed). She could laugh now about her fright at the house, and assure us again her health need cause no real alarm. Comfortably settled on her pillows, she kissed Nina goodbye and sent her love to Alan waiting downstairs: they had to start back to collect Jonquil, 'farmed out' to a friend. I waved from the window as Alan's car left.

Very much I wished there had been a chance to talk privately to Alan. It didn't happen because my mother wanted me beside her all the time. Nor was there any chance to pour out my thoughts to Steve, for he had melted away while we were getting the invalid to bed. Presently I looked vainly all round for him. At dinnertime I ate in my mother's room, a service helpfully arranged by Sea Winds.

Later, after she dropped asleep, I sought Steve yet again. Tonight heavy clouds were banking, the air was breathless and sultry. 'A storm coming,' old Mrs. Pike prophesied, 'is that what made your poor dear Mum take bad?'

Might Steve have walked down to the sea for some coolness? I went to that part of the beach we called 'ours'. Over the darkening sea was an ominous rumble. He wasn't there.

As I turned slowly back, the hotel lights glimmered through a premature dusk. A few people were around, in the bar and the lounge, but not Steve. Nor Willard, as though that mattered to me.

But it did a moment later. As I wandered past the small 'library', equipped with bookshelves and a few tables and seats, the door stood ajar and a voice came out to me — so familiar and yet so changed, because I had never heard it raised in a passion to rival the mounting storm outside.

I couldn't catch the torrent of words, lent by excitement a much more pronounced foreign intonation. But plainly I heard Willard's half-angry, half-soothing response, 'Just simmer down, will you? — there's no need for us to fall out like this, Steve, none at all! — '

Then the door moved under my hand, bringing sudden quiet. Willard turned hastily from his seat at a table.

'Ruth! I'm glad you've interrupted us before this stupid argument gets out of hand!'

I mumbled, 'Argument?'

'You didn't hear, then? — no? Oh, just about the garden — and I still say rhododendrons will never thrive in that soil!' He laughed, quite good humouredly. 'Never mind, if Cecily has her roses she'll be happy. How is she feeling now?'

I said she was sleeping, and he nodded. It had been an unfortunate day, he sympathised. Would I care for some coffee, or something stronger to steady my nerves?

More or less politely, I refused both.

'I think I'll get a drink, if you'll both excuse me. No hard feelings?' he asked Steve as he left us. Steve echoed curtly, 'No hard feelings!'

I looked across at him, standing by the window, his face still dark with anger.

'Whatever was all that about?'

'Rhododendrons, the man said. You heard him!'

'Was that all? Steve, where were you all this time? — only I've so much to tell you, I don't know where to start! — '

'Sorry, will it keep a while?'

I stared at him. For so long I had held my urgent tale in check, and now I found the warmth of him all turned to distant coolness. I tried to ask, 'Is something wrong?'

Lightning wavered on the window, reflecting on that moody face, all at once a stranger's. He said, 'No! Storms make me nervous. I'm going to bed.'

He was actually walking out of the room with no other word. Then he paused just to touch my cheek with lips as chill as his abrupt 'Good night!'

He was as eager to leave me as he had been all these hours to avoid me. I tried to delve back through this difficult day, but I couldn't think when the change began. Surely not since he renewed acquaintance with my sweet-faced sister? . . .

I went to bed early myself, though the idea of sleep seemed impossible. And indeed, my eyes scarcely closed, between the sullen beat of rain and remembering my mother screaming in a darkened cellar. When daylight came I was glad to get up.

She was looking tired too, but thankfully much more herself, determined to go down with me for breakfast. As we sat down, a low voice behind my chair murmured, 'Ruth?'

I looked round at the penitent waver of a dimpled smile. Steve whispered, 'Sorry about the bad temper. I'm sorry.' He asked my mother quietly about her health today. He acknowledged Willard, ''Morning, nice weather for rhododendrons, Mr. Enderby?'

Willard said urbanely, 'Haven't we exhausted that topic, Mr. Stenning?'

Before seeking his own place, Steve whispered to me again, 'See you later, please?'

However, that 'later' wasn't to be yet — for I was still spooning in cornflakes when my mobile phone jangled. Hastily I excused myself. The call was from Alan.

Out in the quiet garden I almost babbled, 'Oh, I'm so glad to speak to you! Mum does seem better today — but I was going to ring you about yesterday! — '

It was 'yesterday' he wanted to discuss. That recent quarrel of ours obviously forgotten, for once Alan the maddeningly cautious was ready to speak straight out. What I had sensed at the old house was true: it had taken those moments of melodrama to convince him, but now he shared my belief that there could be more to Willard Enderby than met the eye.

And the workings of Alan's mind went even further.

'Ruth, last Sunday didn't you say

Steve has a bed-sit at Clovelly Place, Ealing? I've checked up. There's no such road.'

'Then I misheard him. Does it matter? — we've got to talk about 'dear Will' — '

'I'm coming to 'dear Will'. Let me do this my own bumbling way. You see, I agree Mr. Enderby could be working a clever scam — with a professional touch, not like a first-time amateur. But hardly a one-man show. He needs an equally clever accomplice.'

I echoed just that last word. '*Accomplice?*'

'Think about it. Someone to clear his way by diverting the attention of meddlesome relatives — which means you, I'm afraid. Someone on the spot, using whatever method would work best, to handle any inconvenient suspicions. This time, planted at the hotel pretending to be a private investigator, all eager to help — but really ensuring you don't call in any real investigators who'd be a danger to the pair of them.'

I breathed, 'Alan!' He went relentlessly on.

'Involving you in a — hem! — a 'holiday romance' would be part of the scheme, to keep you occupied. And behind the scenes, all your confidences are passed straight to Willard by his sidekick, so they can keep one jump ahead — do you see? — '

'I won't listen! It — it's the most impossible, stupid idea I've ever heard! Just because you've never liked Steve, you've always been downright jealous! — '

The voice across the miles was still composed.

'It's true I haven't trusted him, but not without cause. Remember when I suggested Robert Collyer might oversee your mother's finances, who squashed that right away? And yesterday at the house, Steve was first to rescue her — but why was he on the spot at the crucial moment? I was watching him ... he could very easily have turned off the lights and fastened the cellar door . . . '

I almost wailed, 'That's not true! It's utter rubbish!'

Not true, all my senses and instincts cried out in pain and horror, never true of the man whose face and voice filled my dreaming and my waking! Not true he could so cruelly have deluded me, that the closeness so precious could be only a mirage, a living lie!

'Anyway,' I exclaimed in sudden triumph, 'hasn't he just found out for me about Beatrice Withers? You know he did!'

'Yes. Quite safe, when your Mum already knew. And pretending he'd 'found it out' would make you trust him all the more.'

I gave a little moan. Without that I had trusted him, without even our long days together, the moments he held me in his arms. I had even laughed at myself, clear-headed Miss Stafford, forsaking my safe terra firma for painted pink clouds and tinsel stars. I wasn't laughing now.

'All right.' I drew a deep breath. 'If you're so clever, if it's true, then prove it! Go on and prove it!'

'I'm so sorry to put you through this. But for your mother's sake — please, just think hard. Isn't there one tiny hint of a liaison between Willard and Steve? You're there with them. You have a very perceptive mind.'

He was actually expecting me to provide his proof! I said shortly, 'A liaison? — you must be joking! They hate the sight of one another!'

'They may give that impression when you're around. All part of the act.'

'It's no act, they argue when I'm not around! Last night I overheard them really quarrelling, and Willard said, 'Simmer down, Steve, there's no need to fall out like this!' — '

I stopped there, as if someone else had spoken those words and let the truth of them burst through. Alan prompted softly, 'Say that again? When they thought they were alone, Willard called him — ?'

'He said 'Steve'. Yes he did, I heard him! Only — ' My voice collapsed into something like a sob. 'I — I just didn't realise it then . . . '

'Of course not,' Alan tried anxiously to comfort me.

Almost beyond my consciousness, his voice still spoke. One little slip, he said, perhaps enough on its own to rescue my mother, perhaps enough to prove two wily plotters were not quite infallible.

Later, I might know the bitterness of humiliation, the fire of futile anger. At this moment, I knew only pain.

4

I had rushed outside to speak to Alan, but I returned very slowly. The bustle of the hotel was all around, morning sun at the windows. To my eyes it had become a grey waste.

Alan had been very kind, warning me we must lie low, plan ahead as shrewdly as the two schemers. I mustn't question Steve, to send him straight to Willard so they could take precautions. I mustn't yet tell my mother.

Mercifully, the documents Willard's lawyer was bringing here today — the new will, the papers concerning the house — were in draft form to be agreed, so we had a respite. Alan would see his legal friend, Robert Collyer, for advice. And meantime it would be my own almost impossible task to play along with Steve as though I suspected nothing. In misery, I promised that I would try.

Alan was full of anxious sympathy. If I had treated him badly, I was paying for it now.

My mother greeted me, 'Well, you two had a long talk! Ruthie, this Mr. Leigh-Somebody will be here for lunch with those tiresome documents, but that's no reason to spoil your day. You look tired, how about a picnic or a little coach ride?'

I chose neither. When I went out, it was in Steve's car.

He sought me out shortly before the solicitor was due. There was a Flower Show in Brighton, he said, and we could have lunch there. 'Or did you want to attend this legal get-together?' he asked, the young, smooth forehead creasing. 'I daresay old Enderby won't welcome you, but you could try gate-crashing.'

'Today doesn't really matter. When it gets to signatures, that'll matter.'

Uncannily he echoed Alan's words. 'Yes, it gives us a respite. Meantime

— the sky is blue again for us — ' The twin dimples deepened. 'I cleaned out the car this morning just for you, to make up for my bad tantrums last night. So shall we hit the road?'

I could hardly look at him, I could scarcely speak to him. Almost desperately I wanted to refuse his wheedling invitation. I had given Alan my solemn promise, but this very first trial showed how incredibly hard it would be to keep. In the end, I agreed without protest: if indeed Steve's aim was to steer me out of Willard's way, he succeeded hands down.

The Flower Show in one of Brighton's Parks displayed for us its rainbow glories. The sky, freshened by last night's rain, smiled on us. To other eyes, the sea would still be blue.

Steve chose a restaurant to buy me a lunch I could scarcely swallow. He joked about the flowers we had just seen — 'Got to do my homework for Monsieur Big-Head Enderby, he still thinks R. Stenning is a blundering fool!

. . . What was it you tried to tell me last night? Was it about your mother? — you know I'll do anything to help . . . '

I didn't know, not any more. And this kind of pantomime wasn't for me, if I couldn't face him outright with an accusation of double-dealing then each moment of pretence was an agony!

What explanation I gave for last night's anxiety, I hardly knew: something about the potential value of The Old Lodge — and he agreed seriously, 'Yes, I was surprised when I saw it.' If he noticed nothing strange in my manner, perhaps that was because he too seemed preoccupied today.

But I could endure the strain only so long. I pleaded, 'Sorry, I've such a bad headache. Could we go back early?'

Then he was all sympathy and concern. And I could have hit myself for ever doubting him, I could have hit him too for giving me so much cause.

It was almost five when we got back. Striped sunshades blossomed on the terrace, curtains stirred at open windows. This was the moment I had dreaded, the gentle hand turning my face towards his, the caressing lips finding mine. The arms around me were warm and wonderful, even now they were.

For how could I remain unmoved, when I still couldn't imagine my life without him? The restless spirit so far from my own, the voice and the smile and the touch of him I loved, the tenderness and the laughter! The fall of dark hair on his forehead, the eyes innocent as a child's, or wickedly teasing, or inscrutable as midnight!

'I love you, Steve!' almost I cried aloud. 'I love you, I love you! — so tell me this horrible thing isn't true, it's just a ghastly mistake — '

I didn't say it. I closed my eyes and I clung to him.

'Ahem!' My mother coughed loudly, peering into the car. 'You're back then, children! I'm sure you've had a better time than I have. A lot of gibberish these lawyers talk!'

Steve asked quietly, 'Was it all settled, Mrs. Stafford?'

'Oh yes, dear. I just need to sign the final papers when they're ready.'

My own voice said, from miles away, 'So when will that be?'

'About a week. Only a week.'

I went inside with her. She was chattering on about a shopping spree to buy me a lovely outfit for the wedding — and Nina too, of course. And what sort of flowers would I suggest? I didn't, of all things, want to think about flowers.

Most of all I needed a chance to phone Alan. It came later that evening, again out in the garden. I told him, 'Only a week!'

'I see. Well, I haven't wasted time. I've seen Robert — he and his wife have a new bungalow — and Nina came too, to look after Joni while we talked business — '

I remembered Robert Collyer, previously in the Legal Section at the Estates

Company: bespectacled, slow-spoken and serious. In some ways he and Alan were two of a kind.

'Robert took a serious view. Of course, we need some hard facts, but — ' For an instant he paused. 'As soon as your mother signs those documents — there's just a chance, just an outside chance, her life could be put at risk.'

That utterly hideous thought had come to me before, and I had thrust it aside But now these responsible men had come to the same conclusion. Hard though it was to believe anyone would operate this cold-blooded plan . . . totally impossible to believe it of Steve! . . .

'You do understand?' Alan asked gently. 'Robert wants to talk to you, we'll fix up something. Meantime, we'll do all the checking up we can. And one other thing — ' Again came that hesitation over difficult words: when they came, they shook me as much as his brutally frank suggestion a moment ago.

Mr. Collyer wished to bring in, even if informally at first, a friend of his experienced in such matters. The friend's name was Sutcliffe. Hugh Sutcliffe. Or, officially, Detective Inspector Sutcliffe.

I was near to panic now. This whole thing was snowballing out of control. I said shakily, 'I know we must stop them, but — not the police, not if — if Steve . . . Please, let me warn him! Oh, he might run straight to Willard — but then won't they just vanish into the blue, not bother us again?'

'Not us, maybe. But — the next defenceless victim?'

He was right, of course. I mumbled, 'People who're caught doing these things — ' I didn't need to specify, profiting by their sharp wits without scruple or pity. 'They usually end up in jail, don't they?'

'That's the risk they take. I know your Mum would be very upset for 'dear Will', but when she understands I'm sure she'll get over it.'

Again, he was right. But he must have known I wasn't worrying about Willard, nor even at this moment about my mother.

We said goodbye. We promised to keep in touch.

'I know we must stop them!' I cried out just now. Was there any defence for the man who was bringing me such heartbreak? It wouldn't be my fault if retribution caught up with him, if this soaring, endearing bird — a brightly plumaged bird from foreign climes — ended up with those colourful wings clipped.

I recalled a moment on the cliff-top, he and I under white skating clouds — and those impassioned words of mine, 'Cruel tricksters like that deserve to be behind bars for a long, long time!'

I hadn't dreamt what I was really saying. But he knew. I remembered the dark eyes that puckered and fell.

★   ★   ★

'Mum, can I speak to you seriously?'

I asked the question over tea and home-made cake in The Old Forge Tea-Garden. For two nights and a day I had wrestled with my private turmoil and my game of pretence. Today, welcoming Willard's absence 'on business', I had inveigled my mother on to a bus and out here to see an old village church famed for some Blacksmith's Grave legend: a quiet retreat to talk to her undisturbed.

We had seen the churchyard and bought a souvenir. Now, the time was ripe to have my say. And I had to find the right words, before it was too late to halt a rolling snowball in its tracks.

'Mm, nice cake, dear,' she was mumbling through a mouthful. 'Like your Grandma's recipe, she made them every Sunday. — What were you saying, Ruthie?'

It wasn't easy to get all her attention. I leant towards her across the rustic table.

'You won't like this, but — ' I

stopped, and then plunged. 'Listen, you had the shock of Aunt Charlie's legacy, then you found out you weren't well. You've been upset, not really yourself! And is that the time to decide a huge thing like getting married? You know Nina and I will always look after you, live anywhere, do anything! If — if only you'll think again and change your mind? — '

There was hurt now in her face, as well as quite a bright anger.

'Now that's enough! I'm really disappointed in you, being so obstinate! I hoped getting to know Will better would stop these silly jealous ideas of yours.'

Almost I shouted at her, 'Not again!'

'Of course we've all been happy together,' she went on a little more calmly. 'But we'll be more so with dear Will part of the family. I know things can't ever be the same as when poor Daddy was alive — but Will is a fine man, a dear kind man. A man you can trust!'

I choked quite unintelligibly. There were tears in my eyes.

'So please, don't let's argue,' she urged. 'Why not think of your own future? Give Alan a nudge, and fix up a nice little wedding? If we're speaking so plainly, you know it's been bothering me to see you getting so embroiled with young Ray. It's nice you're having fun here, but — wouldn't it be a shame to risk hurting Alan?'

I said gruffly, 'We're discussing your wedding, not mine.'

'Alan and you make a perfect pair,' she insisted earnestly. 'So now your old Mum is off your hands, live your own life. Don't let time slip away from you!'

This time one of those tears fairly plopped down on to my plate. I tried one last plea. 'I'll think about it — if you'll do one thing. Wait a while before you decide about the house or the marriage, just to be quite sure Will is all you think he is.'

She wagged a finger at me. 'I *won't* have you say bad things about him! If that's why you brought me here, I'll get straight on a bus back again!'

In her hurt indignation she might have done just that, if I hadn't suddenly detected a movement behind the leafy hedge dividing our table from the quiet village road. I exclaimed, 'What's that? — Who's there?'

A voice protested, 'Now you've spoilt my surprise. I was just going to impersonate a dangerous escaped bull.'

'It's Ray!' My mother laughed in relief that our argument had been ended. 'Did you see the Blacksmith's Grave too? — do have some tea with us, dear, the cakes are yummy!'

How long had Willard's spy been there, how much of our talk would be conveyed to Willard's ears? Had he heard me suggest this outing and kept watch on us all afternoon? As he opened the gate I looked up at him, and quickly looked away.

I said hardly a word, but my mother was quite her bright self again. When finally we left, it wasn't to get the bus.

Steve had his car on hand. Maybe he tailed our bus on the way out, I thought grimly, a cloak-and-dagger antic that would appeal to him!

'Will you sit in front with me, Madame?' he invited my mother. 'Not too close. That delightful perfume you're wearing might distract my driving.'

She scolded, 'You're exactly the sort of bad lad my old Gran used to warn me about.'

While they enlivened the drive with more badinage, I huddled on the back seat, longing for the journey to end. Before it did, Steve had asked her, 'As a reward for the ride, could I borrow Ruth again this evening? She might like the 'whodunnit' at the Alhambra.'

'Oh yes, she loves cops-and-robbers stories! You both go, have a good time,' she agreed readily. 'Only I ought to tell you, Ray — you won't take offence, dear? — my Ruth is very nearly engaged. You've met Alan, haven't you? I just don't want anyone getting hurt.'

He said quietly, 'You're a very gracious lady, Mrs. Stafford.'

If he truly thought that, how in heaven's name could he sit beside her, look into her earnest face — and not hide his own face in shame?

Quite desperately I didn't want to go out with him tonight! I rehearsed all sorts of excuses, but the time went by and I didn't make them. At dinner he waved to us extravagantly across the room, and Willard raised a disapproving eyebrow.

Afterwards, Steve was waiting for me. All the more I berated myself for not saying 'No!' Still more fiercely for choosing this outfit I hadn't worn before — the clingy top, the swirl of filmy black skirt scattered with silver embroidery, even a sparkly clip in my hair! What sort of idiot was I?

Whether the play was good or bad, I didn't know, for I could pay no heed to fictional 'cops and robbers'. Reality was more than enough. When we left the theatre the sky was dark, the air balmy and languid: a late-evening panorama moved around us, women with bare sun-bronzed shoulders, men in bright holiday shirts, a few overtired children clamouring for a last ice-cream. Young couples strolled entwined.

I let Steve take my hand, as he always did. Passively I walked at his side through the Esplanade Gardens, their dim flowerbeds and waterfalls turned by tinted lights to fairyland.

It was quiet here. The seat by the pool was quieter still. He reached over to pluck a little white flower, offering it to me in an exaggerated accent, 'Ze compliments of ze Parks Department, Ma'mselle.'

I couldn't answer. The time and place, the nearness of him, had brought back those tears that had plagued me all day.

He said suddenly, quite sharply, 'Don't look at me like that!'

I faltered, 'Like — what?' I was shivering. I trembled scarcely less when his arm quickly encircled me.

'With that sadness in your eyes. It breaks my heart to see you cry. Oh, I know I shouldn't say this — straight after your mother gave me her kind warning — but I have to tell you! I love you so much . . . there aren't words to say . . . I've loved you since we first met, even then we weren't strangers — you remember that? — '

I remembered. Dear heaven, I remembered!

'And now you're so unhappy, so worried. So won't you let me rescue you from these troubles? You've done all you can for your Mum, I'm sure now it will come out right! And I'll make you happy, I swear to you, if you'll say one little 'yes' . . . if you'll marry me, Ruth?'

I tried to turn my head away, not to see, not to hear. But how quickly and eagerly he would have had his answer if I could believe one word he was telling me! If the truth weren't so cruelly plain, that any glowing mirage he would offer, any empty promise, to steer me clear of the Enderby master-plan!

'I know I don't deserve you,' still he was persuading softly. 'You have a future all lined up, I've no right to intrude on it. I'm not proud of my life: always I drift and drift — not all my own fault but much of it. But with you help, I'll do better. I'll make for you a happy future, I swear to you . . . '

There was still a pure-white flower crushed in my hand. So perfectly he knew how to set his stage. So expertly this face that would haunt all my days missed no beseeching earnestness, this voice no break or tremor. Indeed, with such talent, his name — whatever was his name! — should grace theatre façades for years to come!

Except that his tomorrow would hold no cheers and curtain-calls: those soulful eyes would look instead upon the grim realities of arrest and trial for conspiracy, for fraud — even, if I dared think of it, for worse. All drawing nearer, every moment nearer, unless I warned him. Unless I broke my vow to

Alan, I endangered others as my dear mother was endangered — or unless, please God, these terrible suspicions still could somehow be proved wrong? . . .

'Oh, Steve!' I whispered. It came out like a sob, and I felt his arm tighten. 'I — I don't know. I don't know what to say. I need — more time!'

Time to seek the truth, time to stall and keep on stalling, to continue this agonizing game of pretence. I caught my breath in a laugh not far from hysteria.

'You certainly don't wait around, do you? Do you always say these things to girls you've known a whole fortnight?'

He silenced me then with his lips on mine. I had to let him kiss me, and hold me, and rock me gently like a small frantic child needing to be soothed.

'Don't mock me. You shall have time to answer. But please, one answer now — say you love me just a little? Tell me you do?'

My face was against his, my eyes were closed. I heard my own voice say,

'You know I do. You know, Steve.'

'No, not 'Steve' this time. Please, sa[y] my name to me?'

Was it still my voice, obedientl[y] speaking the words it had to speak? ' love you . . . Raoul, I do love you . . .

There were people walking past u[s] The world was still going on. A stirrin[g] of night breeze carried my words awa[y]

'Come on,' he said gently. 'Let's g[o] back.'

★ ★ ★

It was on Thursday that Willard arrive[d] late for breakfast — he had no busines[s] commitments that day — and hande[d] me a letter he had just picked up i[n] Reception.

'For you! Is that your sister's writing What has little Nina to say for herself[?]

The mere thought of his handlin[g] that missive made my blood run col[d] Whatever Nina had committed t[o] paper, it wouldn't be for his eyes!

I had been worrying about Nin[a]

Each time I phoned she was out — which in itself was unlike her. Just once I reached her, late on Tuesday, and then she was at Alan's house, doubtless helping with Jonquil: she seemed tongue-tied, in a rush to say goodbye.

I knew my sister well, a transparent, susceptible soul. I believed I knew what ailed her. If she had succumbed to a pair of dark melting eyes and a soft intimate voice, could I of all people blame her? Maybe she too had tried to dissuade Alan from 'letting justice take its course.'

And now had come this letter, already almost public property. It was to her credit that her mind wasn't attuned to intrigue and subterfuge.

'Do read it out, Ruthie!' my mother was pressing. 'The poor love hasn't got one of her summer 'flu things?'

I was scanning the lines of small neat handwriting:

'Just to say I gave Alan the message you phoned through, that Mum and

Mr. Enderby are signing the legal papers on Monday morning at the house . . . Alan says, don't worry, he's coming with Mr. Collyer and also Mr. Collyer's friend who'll be helping them . . . '

Why didn't she just shout from the rooftops that this 'friend' was also a policeman?

I said carefully, 'She doesn't mention 'flu. She's seen Alan. And — '

At this point a sleight-of-hand trick upended my glass of fruit juice neatly into my lap. I fled upstairs to change, the letter clutched in my hand.

Safe in my room, I tried to calm my taut nerves. I couldn't stand much more of this! The rest of Nina's words didn't help much:

'We think you're WONDERFUL, all you're doing for poor Mum. I could never do it. I'll see you on Monday at the house, I'll be there too, but won't it be an awful, awful day? . . . '

She didn't mention Steve. I tore the paper into fragments. By rights I should have swallowed them.

'An awful day', she prophesied. But could it be worse than my agony of waiting for it, playing out this ghastly charade? Would Alan be too upset if I took matters into my own hands? — because I had to do something, I had to!

In the afternoon my moment came. My mother was occupied in the library, making notes for sending out wedding invitations. On the terrace Willard was working too, with his 'lap-top' and a file of papers. For a moment I watched him from a distance: the dark blazer with some sort of badge, the face lean and bronzed contrasted by silvered hair. A fine-looking man, you had to concede.

My courage was pumped up as high as it would ever be. I joined him at his table.

He greeted me, 'Just enjoying the sun, Ruth? Or did you want to talk to me?'

I mumbled I was waiting for Ray, we were going down to the beach. Meeting those shrewd Enderby eyes, I prayed the wait wouldn't be long. Luckily, we hadn't progressed beyond comments on the weather when I saw Steve looking round for me, and beckoned.

'Afternoon, Ray! You young people are off for a swim, are you?' Willard's cordial voice had chilled just a fraction.

'We are. Can't we tempt you, Mr. Enderby?' Steve invited gravely.

'A few years back, you needn't have asked me twice. Well, have fun, both of you!'

I wasn't accepting dismissal just yet, after contriving this uneasy threesome.

'Oh, there was something I wanted to say. Mum seems worried about The Old Lodge garden, I wondered if anything has been settled yet? Only, didn't you disagree about it rather violently with — *Steve?*'

I said that name very clearly, and then I waited.

The first reaction was Steve's, a sharp warning nudge. From Willard came only a puzzled murmur, 'I beg your pardon, my dear?'

That was all. Just that. Steve quickly filled in the silence, 'The best thing for Mrs. Stafford to do is browse through some nice coloured catalogues. I'll see she has some.'

I let him pick up my beach bag. I walked with him away down the drive. Safely clear of Willard's table he whistled a long, dramatic 'Phew!'

'I'm sorry about that.'

'Let's not panic! I don't think the old boy paid much attention.'

He smiled his dimpled smile, quite serenely. My 'test' had failed dismally, of course. Either the two of them genuinely shared no dark secrets, or they were both equally competent actors. I was no nearer discovering which.

On the beach we found a few families encamped on towels and chairs. Never much of a swimmer, today I launched out boldly, in the hope that swimming might prove safer than talking. It didn't, because my progress lapsed into a submerged gurgle, and Steve glided across to salvage me. I clung limpet-like round his neck, unable to avoid a watery kiss. There were more ways than one to get out of your depth.

Back ashore, as I huddled on a large pink towel determined not to leave it again, he rummaged out a postcard and passed it to me to read. I thought, not Nina! But then I recognised the childish handwriting:

'Hello, Thanks for my swiming lesson and I did a hole width in the big Baths, didn't we have fun, love to you and Auntie Ruth from Jonquil.'

Something contracted in my throat, preventing words. Nor did Steve speak, for so long that I looked round at him — and was startled by rare frown-lines transforming and ageing.

He said as though I had spoken, 'Yes,

I know. I'm selfish to want you for myself when this little one with no mother wants you too.' His voice was only a whisper. 'But I need you so much, Ruth. You are — a bright guiding star.'

I mumbled foolishly, 'I — I am?'

There was sand in my hair, and the sun on my face. The salt blurring my eyes wasn't all from the sea.

5

I was acquiring a very nice tan, as if that mattered. I was still tying my long hair in a tail, or even letting it flow loose, instead of coiling up the severe knot I invariably wore at work. After that rather disastrous swimming session, I arrived for lunch maybe looking about nineteen — and feeling nearer ninety.

As we ate, Willard was pointing out graciously how much space there would be at The Old Lodge for us all if Nina and I chose to make it our home. (It wasn't yet his to be so free with, but that was a minor detail.) Of course, my mother beamed delighted approval. Afterwards he took her for a drive — and I went along too, to avoid being with Steve.

When we arrived back, Mum went to lie down a while. Willard was still lingering in the car, studying something on a map. Desperation was driving me on, and I still wasn't beaten, not quite yet. I joined him to thank him politely for the ride.

'My pleasure, Ruth!' He inclined his well-groomed head.

'It's nice country round here. But I'm not sure I'll need a home at The Old Lodge — or maybe not for long. You see, I've had a proposal of marriage.'

'Well!' He laid down the map, with every appearance of cordial pleasure. 'I'm delighted! I told your mother how well you and Alan seem to be suited.'

'Not Alan,' I corrected. 'Ray Stenning. I haven't answered him yet, I haven't even told Mum. But — I'm thinking about it.'

At long last, I had won a reaction from this cool, clever man! Before his composure came quickly back, I saw surprise and displeasure — and even alarm?

Not that I wanted any of those, if

they signified shock at finding his young partner had so much overplayed staging merely a brief holiday affair, causing annoying complications. But why else should he care whether or not I wanted to marry Steve?

'Er — perhaps you'd sit down a moment,' he was inviting.

Whatever I expected next, certainly it wasn't words earnest and reasonable enough to shake even my fixed and fervent convictions.

'I find this rather disturbing. I'm sure if your father were alive he'd say this better — but sadly he's not. So can I speak to you plainly? Sometimes an observer sees more of a situation than people too close to it. I'm afraid if you rush into this marriage you'll live to regret it.'

I protested, 'I'm not rushing, just thinking!'

'Of course, that's like you. Especially when this doesn't only involve yourself, we both know Cecily mustn't be caused unnecessary worry.'

My guard was slipping. I said defiantly, 'What's so wrong about marrying him?'

'I'm not saying it's 'wrong' — but I really can't believe he's the right match for a steady-minded girl like you. And you'd be most unwise to ditch someone of Alan Blakely's merit on the spur of the moment. You've known this young fellow really no time at all, have you? I've no idea how old he is — '

'Younger than I am! Is that a problem?'

'No. But his happy-go-lucky, devil-may-care attitude to life might be. And he does seem to have some sort of — er, Latin temperament — you'll know more of his background than I do — which might cool down away from all this sun and seaside! So — ' He cleared his throat, as though he wasn't enjoying this. 'Suppose I have a little word with him — as the Victorians would say, to find out his intentions?'

'I don't know about that,' I objected.

'I'll be very discreet, I promise! You

know, the world isn't always a pretty place. I don't want you to discover that the hard way.'

I blinked and swallowed and groped. This must be just his way of countering Steve's out-of-line behaviour? Surely, it would be too absurd to take him at his word? And still he had another knot to add to the tangled skein.

'One more thing, my dear. I've noticed him paying some of his own brand of attention to Nina. Enough to turn her pretty little head, I fancy.'

He had seen that too, it was that obvious! Unless — his idea was to set sister fighting sister like cats instead of meddling in our mother's affairs. I couldn't hide now how deeply I was shaken and confused. I mumbled I would 'think things over', and almost ran for the seclusion of my own room.

So much for my second brave bid to uncover the truth! More than ever I was sickened — for Nina now as well, who had harmed no-one in all her gentle life. For her sake there stirred some-thing I hadn't yet felt for my own, anger against Steve fierce and stern, if this were truly the man looking out of those teasing eyes!

And there still remained the need to get through these remaining hours of waiting without breaking my pledge of silence. It seemed a hopeless task, until I thought of a way out.

Not just that evening, but all through Friday and Saturday, I kept to my room. When my mother diagnosed a bad headache (yes, I certainly had one!) as 'too much sun', I didn't dispute it, and rested meekly in the shaded room with a cold damp flannel on my brow. Perhaps a cowardly way out, but sneaky people demanded sneaky methods.

Not that this seclusion hadn't its problems, for Steve haunted my door to push under it notes and get-well cards, and sent in via my mother gifts of fruit and flowers. '*Toujours a toi*' stated the note attached to one posy. Charming, except it didn't specify whether his loyalty was to me, to my sister, or to puppet-master Enderby pulling all the strings. I wanted to fling those flowers back at their donor. Equally, I wanted to collapse into his arms.

Between whiles Mum brought snippets of news. The wedding invitations were going out, a little reception was being planned. 'Dear Will' was helping her order furnishings and carpets for the house. Though not by nature a fatalist, I was nearing despair.

It was Sunday morning when I was roused from this dismal inactivity, by such a simple thing, just a glance from my window. I was up and dressed, because I knew it was time I started to recover: and then I looked out at the garden — and saw Steve pursuing old Mrs. Pike with a magazine she had dropped, sitting beside her with friendly patience to be talked to.

The sun was on his face, the breeze lifting the hair from his forehead. I thought of tomorrow, hours away, when his life would be laid in ruins. After tomorrow, how long had he left to walk in this free sunshine?

The time for passive sorrowing, for futile anger, was over. One stratagem I still had left, avoided until now in sharp distaste. I knew which was his room on the floor above: its door should be fastened, but it might not be, he wasn't over careful. If Mrs. Pike's hospital anecdotes lasted ten minutes (usually they took far longer) it would be enough.

On the landing and the stairs I met no-one. His door wasn't locked, the key flung down carelessly on a chair.

The room was similar to my own, only beige instead of lilac. I began peering and prying, looking through drawers, opening the big shabby suit-case labelled R. STENNING.

I found clothes, books, oddments, only the things you would expect to find — until I unearthed a folder holding some loose papers. A few letters were in scribbled French, but the name 'Raoul' at the top and the signature 'Pierre' were enough, for Steve had mentioned this cousin of his. There were a couple of old family snapshots and some theatre programmes, one with his name in the cast, several with his mother's — the stage-name Francine Rossetti he had mentioned to me. As well, her photograph enclosed in tissue, the likeness in her smile unmistakable ... and a fragment of her handwriting, a faded pressed flower.

I felt as though I had desecrated a shrine. With reverence I replaced them.

But one more thing I couldn't miss seeing, a half-written letter lying openly on the little table. But this wasn't half-understood French, this was unknown Italian. I was holding it, frowning at it, when a sound made me start violently. The door opened.

Steve said only, 'It's you!' He looked as startled as I was. 'Were you looking for me?'

'I — I shouldn't have walked in here — I'm sorry! — '

'It doesn't matter. I'm just so glad you're better. If you weren't downstairs tomorrow I meant to call a doctor to you myself.'

'Did you?' I whispered. I replaced the letter on the table. 'Sorry to be so nosey. I couldn't read a word anyway! Is this for your Grandma in Italy you told me about?'

'No. She died, didn't I tell you that too? I was too late to say goodbye.' He sighed, fluttering the unfinished page. 'But this doesn't answer your question. You see, I still have family there — and suddenly I want to see them again, I lived there when I was small while my mother was busy working. Last night I thought I must go *home*, wherever that is! Only — not all alone.' He said it very simply and wistfully. 'Please, will you come with me?'

Under the window people were talking, laughing, in a world miles away. I made the stark enquiry, 'Is that instead of getting married, or as well as?'

'Do you really have to ask? Can't you believe I'll marry you before we go, when we arrive — today, tomorrow, whenever you want?'

I muttered, 'I see.'

'No, don't say it that way, so cold! I want to show you where I was a child — when my father died and my mother lived for the stage, and this poor sick Grandma gave me so much love . . . and the theatres where my mother played and the audiences so loved her — and the place she met my father, I never knew him but there he seems most real . . . I want you to see it all, so these memories won't be just a solitude . . . '

As always when he was deeply moved or excited, the impeccable English disintegrated a little. I noticed only the loneliness behind the tangled, vivid words.

'It would be nice,' I said softly. 'But travelling around takes money — and you know I can't leave Mum, and — there's my job in London — '

'There'll be other jobs if you want them! The money is no problem, I'll have enough for us — ' If my face was an unspoken question he left it unanswered. 'And your Mum, she'll be married too, she won't need you so much. Oh, I know how you feel about that! — but if she so wants her 'dear Will' it might turn out well? And any time she needs you, do you think I'd keep you from her? I just ask — humbly I ask — spare me a little of your life . . . '

I was looking into his face as though to search out every innermost thought, and I saw pain, longing, even a humility I hadn't seen before. Yet, in pity's name, what could I say to him? That it was a cruel day I ever met him, when to meet him was to love him, so unwisely, so gloriously? That even the disillusion falling since between us like rain from a weeping sky hadn't yet washed that love from my heart?

At this moment, I believed in him. With his eyes on mine almost tearful in their earnestness, I believed, I believed.

'Tomorrow,' I whispered. 'I promise, tomorrow I'll give you an answer.'

He let me free my hands. Those twin dimples deepened at my haste to escape.

'You don't have to run away from me,' he reproached gently. 'Tomorrow, then. So long as this isn't the 'tomorrow that never comes'?'

It would come. It would surely come.

★   ★   ★

I hadn't intended leaving the hotel that day. But after lunch, Alan rang from London, full of concern for my health — and requesting my presence, if I felt well enough, at a last-minute get-together tonight. I promised to meet him, and Robert Collyer, at a station a couple of stops back along the line from Whitedene. I would catch the 7.51.

Meantime I rested on the terrace, my mother vibrating between me and some new arrivals, a pleasant elderly couple.

She was exhibiting photos of The Old Lodge, while Willard looked on indulgently. A long, lazy Sunday, it seemed to be.

Soon after seven I told her I was going out for some evening air. Willard was still beside her, Steve was out in his car.

A bus dropped me at the rail station. The train ride wasn't long: I alighted to see at once a tall familiar figure waiting. Tonight it was hard to look up into Alan's concerned eyes. There was so much I couldn't say to him.

'Good evening, Miss Stafford. I'm afraid you're having an anxious time,' Robert Collyer sympathised. 'I hope we're near to resolving it for you.'

I remembered him well from his days in the Legal Section at work: the precise voice, the thinning hair that had receded further now, the serious face lighted by an unexpected dry humour. I shook hands awkwardly. I let Alan guide me to the Tea Bar, where a bored attendant was starting to clear up for the night.

Three containers of rather turgid tea steamed on a corner table.

'It's nice to see you again,' Robert was saying. 'I'm only sorry about the circumstances. Unfortunately Hugh couldn't be here tonight — '

I echoed, 'Hugh?'

'Hugh Sutcliffe. I've known him years, he was the obvious person to consult. Alan told you, I think?'

Alan had told me. It was just hard to think of D.I. Sutcliffe as 'Hugh'.

'We'll all be at the house tomorrow by eleven. Friends of Alan's interested in such a fine old property, you understand?'

'And before your mother signs anything,' Alan filled in, 'we'll ask some questions 'dear Will' and his sidekick won't like one bit!'

'Alan — ' I struggled to say. I felt my face flame.

'You've done a fine job at your end,' Robert Collyer complimented me. 'Now you can leave the finalities with us. They shouldn't be too difficult now we've uncovered some interesting facts about these bright boys at Sea Winds. For instance, the lad you call 'Steve' — I believe you know him quite well?'

I whispered, 'Quite well.' My hands gripped the table.

'But not so well as you think, I'm sure. He hasn't told you he's the stepson of Mr. Willard Enderby?'

It had to be a dream, some hideous nightmare. I just stared at him. Alan's anxious hand was on my arm, his familiar voice sounding like a stranger's.

'It's true. I'm sorry, Ruth.'

I had never fainted in my life, and this wasn't the moment to begin. I never quite lost my sense of shock and pain, Alan's worried voice asking if there was anything he could do.

Obediently I sipped hot tea. I muttered, 'I'm all right! Just take no notice of me! — and tell me the rest, I want to know it all.'

It was Robert who did most of the telling.

'If he told you he's the son of a car salesman from Birmingham, John Stevenson, and a French/Italian actress known as Francine Rossetti (it does sound an extraordinary pairing!) that much is fact. As for the rest, he isn't, never was, a 'private investigator'. That was an assumed role to stop you making other enquiries.'

'He said — he was at Sea Winds on a case.'

'Naturally! And he let you into the so-called 'secret', very cleverly winning your confidence. Don't blame yourself for being deceived. As to the family relationships, I can confirm Enderby and Francine Rossetti were married — shortly before the lady died when her car ran off a French motor-road. Suspected brake failure, but the car burnt out and nothing was proved.' He produced a news photograph and laid it on the table: I took one glance at the dark, striking face and looked away. 'An attractive woman,' the precise voice said. 'An actress of some talent and success. Very sad. She left a son — Raoul Renato. She also left a will largely in favour of her new husband.'

'But — ' I choked on the words. 'Miss Withers did that too!'

Alan agreed quietly, 'His wives do have a habit of dying on him. But your mother won't be number three.'

I shuddered, even though Robert intervened, 'Well now, Alan, we can't rule out coincidence. In a matter as grave as this we need to curb our imagination.'

I was beyond marvelling at Alan, of all people, being reproved for wild imaginings.

'I'm sorry about Steve,' he was murmuring to me.

'You don't have to be. You can say 'I told you so!' if you want.'

He didn't, of course, just insisting gently that we had now cast-iron proof of Steve's involvement — because he had pretended to us all that his stepfather was a complete stranger. Far more than he did, I knew the extent of the play-acting, the trap spread for me only this morning to lure me away to foreign shores in starry-eyed joy, while whatever Willard planned for my mother was carried out. A scene brilliantly played, that and all the others!

It was pointless now to think back across the time I had known Steve, the idyll and the treachery. One final bitter question tore into me, need he have gone as brutally far as asking me to be his wife? And there was a ready answer, he knew down-to-earth Miss Stafford would embark on no such fairytale jaunts without at least the promise of wedding ring sailing ahead of her!

Mutely my stricken senses cried out to him, You know me too well! . . . *But now I know you. At last I do.*

As for all else that was left to say, just one more thing I was being asked to do. Tomorrow Steve would certainly try to keep me well away from The Old Lodge. But it was essential he must be present, the two conspirators together.

'And if anyone can get him there, it's you,' said the insistent voices.

They didn't specify, would I walk him straight into an ambush, deliver him up to justice with my own hands.

I promised, zombie-like, 'Yes, I'll make sure he's there.'

Alan took me back almost to the hotel. Not quite that far, for it wouldn't do for him to be seen. My mother pounced on me, scolding me for staying out so long and looking 'pale as death'. She insisted on seeing me straight to bed as though I were a child again.

'Tomorrow,' she told me firmly, 'you must have a nice quiet day.'

After her goodnight kiss I lay very still. I shut my eyes and waited for tomorrow.

★ ★ ★

With breakfast finished (other people's, I couldn't touch mine) I was out in the hotel garden. The day was a little overcast, the sun just starting to show. It seemed to me cold as midwinter.

Willard was telling me, 'No need for you to trail along to the house with us, my dear. It's only dull business, and you look tired today.'

But my mother chimed in, innocently in my support, 'Oh, but Will, it would be nice for Ruth to come! Last time I spoilt it by being ill, I won't be so stupid again! It'll be a nice little drive for her.'

'Well,' he smiled at her indulgently, 'if that's what you want, Cecily.'

I wasn't deluded by this easy victory — because now, well on my guard, I was seeing something I must often have missed: an exchange of mute signals, a glance, the barest of answering nods, between Willard and the partner awaiting his orders.

Until this moment I hadn't seen Steve today, but now I had sensed his quiet approach.

'Excuse me,' his voice said startlingly close to me. 'Ruth, there's the Water Gala at the Lido. It might be worth seeing?'

Orders received, orders carried out. I felt a grim triumph in actually watching this pantomime. Willard was objecting, 'Won't it be rather crowded there for Ruth?'

'I'll look after her, Mr. Enderby,' Steve assured him.

They were both looking at me. Willard's glance warned plainly, 'Remember my advice!' Steve's queried, 'Surely you won't let this interfering old fool dictate to you?' Well, this was the last of such games they would play.

I let everyone assume I would go to the Lido. Soon after, I stood by to wave as my mother drove off with Willard, very small and vulnerable beside him in the big car. If I needed a final spur, that glimpse of her was enough.

I went back to find Steve, where two children had drawn him into their game on the lawn. I called to him and he came across to me, his face quickly serious.

'Is something wrong? Oh, this is

'tomorrow' — you've an answer for me?'

'No! No, not that. I couldn't make a scene just now and upset Mum, but you know where they've gone, and why. So I have to be there! Please will you take me?'

He frowned, his mobile hands making one of their wide gestures.

'Must we still worry for her so much? All right, he's marrying her for her money, he's a grasping so-and-so! — but does she care about money? She adores him, so won't she be happy just helping him spend it?'

'I don't want to argue. I have to be there! I was counting on you, I thought you promised you'd do anything to help me.' As the dark, alert eyes met mine I added gruffly, 'But if it's too much bother, I'll get a bus — a taxi — I'll get there somehow!'

'Ruth, I do think you'll just stir up a lot of trouble. But if you want so much to go — for you nothing is a bother. Of course I'll take you there.'

I walked shakily beside him to the car-park. If he would be angry, protest or argue, it might be easier. This way he was going to break my heart — yet again.

The sun was breaking through more and more as we set out, lighting the summer fields and hedgerows sliding past. Steve was unusually quiet, and for half the journey we scarcely spoke. I watched his face, intent and serious — until on a steep hill he made a grimace as the engine coughed and died. We coasted to a standstill.

'So sorry,' he said. 'I'll see what's wrong.'

As he lifted the green bonnet I even believed in some mechanical hitch. I still believed it when a passing driver called to him, 'Need a hand, mate?' and was answered, 'No thanks, we'll be okay.' It actually took me a while to realise a breakdown was a cast-iron certainty between the hotel and The Old Lodge!

'I'm so sorry. I might be able to fix it

but it'll take time . . . ' Who wouldn't have sworn he was genuinely dismayed? 'Is it worth going on if we're too late? We could run back downhill to that garage in the village. We'll still be all right for the Lido.'

'You do that if you want. I'll start walking! Or I'll thumb a lift.'

He muttered something about dubious strangers picking up stranded young ladies. Few of them could be more dubious than he was.

Of course, I didn't need to start walking. My determination had got through to him. So some more poking and prying in the engine saw us on the move again. I commented, 'Amazing what you can do when you try,' and then wished I had kept quiet. Quite conceivably, his next delaying tactic could be to pile us up against a handy tree-trunk?

And in him I had trusted totally, to him given a love beyond understanding! Indeed, it was more like some wild insanity I had suffered — except that such a sickness might be cured, but for this ailment of mine there seemed no remedy in heaven or on earth. For I knew it wasn't cured yet, even by so much hurt and disillusion. Not when I sat here close beside him, trembling as the wheels ate up these fateful miles. Not while I watched in misery his hands on the wheel, the hands I had held and caressed.

In all good faith I had promised Alan to do what must be done. But for me this was a task impossible, a choice impossible — to break my word to a man I trusted beyond question, or stab in the back one I still so crazily loved but would never trust again.

'Are we all right now, cherie?' he was asking me.

I heard myself say, soft and still, 'No, we're not. Shall I tell you why not?'

'Tell me!' he invited.

So I told him. That soft still voice said what it had tried so desperately not to say.

'Because when we get to the house,

you'll find the police there ready fo
you. Because you're just as big a crool
as Willard — and you're his stepson
into the bargain! So now try to lie you
way out of all that!'

6

A moment ago I had feared a contrived accident. Now, I almost brought about a real one. The car veered wildly until Steve reacted to bump it up on to rutted grass at the roadside. Sudden quiet enclosed us.

His face was ashen, his forehead was wet. It seemed an age before he asked, 'How long have you known?'

So denials, plausible explanations, weren't to be forthcoming. I admitted, 'That you're related to Willard, only last night. But we guessed some time ago you were both in league — '

'Who is this 'we'?'

'Alan guessed. I didn't believe it at first. I do now!'

He didn't answer: beyond those two questions he said nothing at all, until I protested with rising warmth, 'Well, where are all the pretty speeches? — in the broken English you turn on to order? Don't say you've run out of words at last!'

He had, it seemed. Obstinately his downcast eyes wouldn't lift. I thought this attitude of a whipped puppy didn't become him — and most of all I sensed sheer anti-climax. After all my agonizing, I had told him the truth. How long was I to sit here while he stared at the floor and thought about it?

I rounded on him suddenly, 'There's just one thing I want to ask you! Whatever that odious man is paying you, do you really think it's worth it? All her life I doubt if my Mum had an unkind thought in her head, she's cared for her family, she lost a husband she adored — she didn't ask to come into money, she'll probably give most of it away! And that's the sort of victim you choose, you and Willard! . . . Steve, are you listening? — '

He was listening. His bowed head drooped still lower as my flood of words poured out: how I understood now the way he had worked himself into my confidence, even how he and Willard appeared cordially to hate the sight of each other. 'And I suppose he told you, 'Make that interfering pest of a girl fall in love with you, just get her out of my hair!' — oh yes, you did that best of all! How much an hour did you get for whispering to me in the moonlight?'

Of that, too, there was no denial. But I wasn't through with him yet, this biggest dressing-down I was ever likely to hand out in all my life.

'Well, I hope you can face living with yourself when Mum is sobbing her heart out — she'll do that before today is over! Or are you hardened to it by now? You've done this sort of thing before, haven't you?'

At least this time I was answered. 'They were — just business deals.'

'Business deals? You mean people you've hoodwinked and robbed — even if their lives weren't threatened like my poor Mum's? Well, she'll live to a fine old age, in her own home on her own

money, in spite of you! And in spite o
her heart problem that won't be so
dangerous if she's not scared to death
before her time! — '

Now, at last, his dark eyes lifted.
blazed on straight into them.

'I never want to see you again afte
today! Sooner or later you'll end up in
jail, that's what you deserve! But I can'
be the one to make it happen, so you'
better get clear now, out of the country
— if your relatives will have you I wish
them joy of you! And — ' I spoilt it al
by trailing off unsteadily, 'I'm such a
fool, I almost hope you get away with i
. . . but I'm sure you won't! . . . '

I could stand no more, struggling to
open the car door. But a hand held me
back.

'Say that again, please! You said — '

'Don't show your face at the house
isn't that plain enough?'

'No, I understand that. About —
your mother's life — ?'

'Her life or her death, was that
another 'business deal'?' I managed to

148

get the door open. 'You tell me, Mr. Stevenson! If she signs that new will today, how much will her life be worth afterwards?'

He didn't tell me, just staring at me, his eyes strangely hollowed.

'Then I'll tell *you*! As much as poor Beatrice Withers' was — she fell on some steps, did she trip, was she pushed? Or your own mother — did her car break down or was it tampered with? And my Mum with her heart trouble, she already had one nasty scare in a dark cellar, how long before she's given a really huge fright somehow? — '

'I don't know what you're saying!' he broke in sharply. 'The stairs — the car — they were accidents — very sad and tragic accidents! — '

'Tragic, yes. Accidents — perhaps. But my Mum won't be the third!'

There were tears streaming down my face now. By some instinct, as I scrambled out of the car, I grabbed up his mobile phone from the front. Then I was running with all my strength, along the lane and away from him. There was a main road ahead, and surely some passing vehicle would stop for me!

But I hadn't reached that road when I heard, above my panting breath, his car coming up behind me — and it swerved dangerously into my path, hemming me in against a spiteful hedge of brambles. Yet I flinched even closer to the thorns when he reached my side.

'Why did you take my phone?' The clear, familiar voice almost surprised me.

'I threw it away, over the hedge somewhere! And if you want mine to warn Willard — you'll have to take it by force!'

'Do you really think I'd do anything to harm you?'

'I don't know! Just — just go away, leave me alone. I promise I won't give you away!'

'You're very kind. That's why I can't drive off and leave you stranded here. Listen, I'll help you! — I'll take you to the house, if we rush we'll still be in time.'

It was a likely story. I said shortly, 'No thanks!'

'Ruth, I swear to you, what you just said about your Mum — I didn't know! I thought she was a sweet foolish woman, I didn't know she was sick! I didn't know!'

A story still more unlikely, one of his skilful blendings of truth and half-truth. I accused, 'Not even on the day you shut the cellar door on her?'

He was frowning in the way that so aged his face. He repeated, 'I didn't know. Willard told me to see the doors were all shut ... afterwards he said she was too excited and had a little faint, just that! ... Oh yes, the money — yes, I admit the money! You called me a thief, a cheat, I own to all of that, to much dirt on these hands! But never to blood, never, never! — I swear before heaven, I swear to you on my mother's grave! — '

They were fine dramatic lines, even for him. I stopped him, 'Don't say

151

things like that! But I hope it's true, fo
your sake.'

'Then let me prove it. There's reall
this trap set up at the house? — ther
we'll go straight there! This rat Enderb
will have no chance to escape —
because now you've opened my eye
I'm willing and eager to serve him up t
them on a plate!'

'How could you do that, when you'r
involved in it too?'

'It's simple. I'll just have to be on th
same plate with him, shan't I?'

Still caught on those brambles,
realised he was deftly unhooking me
He urged, 'Hurry! We'll drive like th
wind!'

Quite unceremoniously I was bundle
into the car. There was little chance t
think or to resist.

I had been fooled, of course — ye
again! It was too late to realise th
incredibility of a man so clever an
devious tamely surrendering himsel
and his partner to justice. Most likel
his aim was to pre-warn Willard, so tw

sets of razor-sharp wits together might evade the tight corner. I was being dragged along too because I knew too much to be left alone.

As for another alternative, I had only his word — whatever that was worth — that we were bound for The Old Lodge at all.

But we were, it seemed. The speedometer rocketed, the landscape whirled by. Just once or twice along the way he asked questions: 'How did you and Alan get on our track?' and 'What exactly has he done about it?' I mumbled some sort of explanations, because I had let too many cats out of bags already to mind freeing a few more.

Through a nightmare haze that had settled on all around, at last a high wall and a wide gateway loomed up. As we lurched to a halt I saw Willard's limousine parked on the driveway, and other cars. A builder's van stood there too, a couple of overalled painters were working on the house. It looked at first glance a busy, peaceful scene.

Already our arrival had been noticed
Alan and Nina came to meet us.

'You've come after all! — Mum said
you were at a Water Show,' my sister
greeted me nervously, fragile and
gold-haired in the sunshine. I didn't
miss the added colour in her face as she
glanced at Steve.

'We changed our minds,' I told her
gently. It was brave of her to be here.

To Alan, standing beside her, what
words could I say? He had worked so
hard for me. He would be grieved and
hurt, he had every right to be furious as
well. I took a deep breath and started
off, 'Alan, I've something to tell
you — '

He didn't hear me, turning aside with
a hasty rebuke, 'Joni! — No, you stay
with me!'

I saw in dismay the child duck past
him and run straight to Steve, to slip
her hand into his. She smiled up at him.
'Hello, did you get my postcard? Can
we go swimming again?'

154

I was sure Steve flinched away from that rapturous greeting. He answered her quietly, 'Sorry, Joni, I think you might have to swim without me.' He let her hand go even before Alan could intervene with rare severity, 'Joni, go and pick some flowers till I call you!'

To me, he muttered, 'School holidays, I had to bring her . . . '

I looked away across a spread of ragged grass to a once fine shrubbery splashed with gold and purple. My mother was chattering away there, out of earshot but the words were evident: 'This will be the rockery, over here the rose-walk — won't it, Will dear? — '

He was nodding urbane agreement. But I looked less at him than the two accompanying guests, dutifully admiring. One was Robert Collyer, grave and formal even here in a sunny garden. His companion was tall, thin, pleasant-faced, and seemed to be sharing a joke with my mother that reduced them both to laughter.

I thought it very unfair of Mr.

Collyer's friend to look so unlike a policeman.

★ ★ ★

As Alan coughed in embarrassment, it might have been amusing, in other circumstances, to see him trying to say what he didn't exactly mean.

'Er — well, Ruth, and — er, Steve . . . Mr. Enderby's lawyer is running late, so we're killing time at present. Mrs. Stafford loves company so I brought two — er, friends along to see the house — '

This was my cue, but no words would come. Amazingly, it was Steve who rescued me.

'Don't strain yourself, Alan! I know about your 'er, friends'. Ruth warned me about the big ambush.'

'Ruth warned you — ?' Alan repeated. Briefly I met his blue astonished eyes.

'Don't blame her,' Steve was ever adding judicially. 'You set her a task

156

much too hard. If you can't see that, you don't know her very well.'

Alan countered sharply, 'Thanks, I don't need you to tell me about Ruth!'

There was an inborn insolence in the answering shrug of Steve's shoulders. It was that, perhaps, that provoked Alan's mild nature beyond all its usual restraint.

'Let me understand this! You had a chance to get away — '

'But he wouldn't take it!' I chimed in. 'He came here to help us!'

'To help us?' Alan rounded quite furiously on Steve. 'You suddenly felt duty bound to assist the course of justice — even if it means walking straight into a prison cell? I've heard some tall tales in my time, but — '

'Sorry, I know it sounds crazy. But ask Ruth, she knows it's true.'

'Ruth is too honest to appreciate a mind like yours!' Alan cut him short. 'You're obviously here to warn Willard, and then Mrs. Stafford will be written off as a near miss and you'll both look out for the next victim. But I'm not letting that happen! Even if I have to drag you to my car and lock you in it — and don't think I can't do it!'

They were face to face, these two men as dissimilar as any could be. Watching, I wondered, had I ever really known either of them? Certainly not Steve, his deceptively youthful face upturned now to Alan's greater height and Alan's resolute words. Nor had I known Alan, so long part of my life but never before a force so compelling — an Alan I hadn't dreamed existed. In admiring respect, I realised how deeply these stillest of waters could run, a storm-tide of anger for me and mine that no wrong to himself could have aroused.

They were Steve's eyes that wavered before this outpouring of scorn. It was Steve who fell back a few strategic steps, as one might who prods an ant and finds it to be a hornet.

It was no-one's fault that this revealing moment ended emptily. Voices were approaching, my mother's in the lead: 'Joni, I wouldn't have known Auntie Ruth was here if you hadn't told me, pet!' They were hurrying towards us, the two visitors tagging on behind. Last of all, Willard Enderby's smile of welcome was genially unruffled.

'Ruthie, I'm so glad you've come!' the excited voice rattled on. 'Such a nice surprise, Nina and Alan coming too — and Alan's friends — and Mr. Collyer says I can have some of his mottled geraniums! . . . '

She went on to perform confused introductions, admonishing Steve, 'Now don't you slip away like a shy violet!' So little she knew what could lie behind a civilized round of handshakes. But I was watching something else: I saw Steve look straight across at Willard, their eyes meeting for a long moment. Was the idea of telepathy too fantastic? Surely they must have some private code, a cough, a nod, a gesture? . . .

'Now do come inside, everyone,' my

mother fluttered. 'It's a real party afte
all!'

It even looked like one, as the house
came suddenly alive with people and
voices, a transformation even greate
than the builders' make-over. I under
stood now the true potential of the
place, that Willard must have seen long
ago.

In the big kitchen, gleaming with new
tiles, my mother was soon busy
organising refreshments, having sen
one of the house-painters to the village
for supplies. Jonquil was happily 'help
ing', while Nina tried patiently to
salvage some order from their chaos.

Still the legal gentleman bringing
those vital documents — a Mr
Leigh-Ferriby, I understood — hadn'
materialised: until he did, we could only
wait. Wait and wonder, for who could
say what had passed between Steve and
Willard at their unavoidable moment of
meeting? Certainly they had been
allowed no contact since. Alan and Mr
Sutcliffe were making a detailed tour of

the house with Willard, holding all his attention. And meantime, along with Robert, I found myself on unbelievable 'guard duty' over Steve in an upper room overlooking the drive.

With surprising docility, Steve hadn't resisted being hustled in here by Alan and told to make no trouble. He even sat meekly on the window-seat as instructed. Mr. Collyer, perched on a packing-case across the door, might have been seated at his own desk. For myself, I kept fidgeting miserably up and down. It was Steve who broke at last this long, impossible pause.

'You know, you won't trap my stepfather this easily. Once before we were in a tight corner — nearly as bad as this — but we came through.'

'I'm bound to say,' Robert cautioned with his dry cough, 'in case you don't realise the gravity of your own position, you should watch what you say.'

'I realise! But I realise too, you've no real evidence yet.' He leant forward confidingly. 'Look, your way you'll give the man a scare, but that's all. Let me handle it my way — let me talk to him — and I'll get you evidence, even confessions from his own lips! And then — *l'affaire est dans le sac!*'

'Quite so. And you're in the sack — er, the bag — too. I can't believe that's your intention. I'd advise you to sit still and be quiet.'

Steve made a face expressing his opinion of that wise counsel.

At that same moment, there was a sound at the door: only Nina, who was peering in with some message from below. As she bent her head near Robert's, I wondered, was this the advent of the belated Leigh-Ferriby at last?

'Ruth? . . . Please? . . . '

I looked round at Steve's urgent whisper. I took a few steps nearer to him.

'I swear I'll play straight with you. Please, persuade them to let me see Willard and I *will* get a confession. I see just how to do it! You know how good I am at staging scenes? — '

I had to assent, 'Well, you can say that again.'

I was looking straight into his face, so innocently imploring — only how often had it been so before? Not an hour ago I vowed never to believe another word he said. Nothing was different.

A sharp refusal was rising to my lips. But then I saw his face change — for both of us heard footsteps on bare boards, and Willard's voice: 'Leigh-Ferriby has made it at last! — so Cecily and I can get our business over with, then she can party to her heart's content! . . .'

Time had run out. It wasn't those words that told me, so much as the sudden unveiled panic in Steve's eyes. His voice wasn't imploring now, it was desperate.

'Ruth, can't you understand? Get him alone, tell him I must talk to him! Tell him — tell him *not to go on with the plan*! Please, you'll do just that for me?'

'Just that', he said. Carry a warning, purely and simply — with now no elaborate fictions disguising the message. This time the charade was over. This time I believed him.

I whispered, 'Don't ask me. Just don't ask!'

But he had asked already. As I backed away, shaking my head, his eyes closed as though in sheer weariness.

Willard was on his way to meet the new arrival. Escaping at last from that miserable room, I watched from a landing window his tall figure stroll on to the drive. I was sick with shock upon shock: even more, knowing that I had just left Steve finally at bay, facing now not only Robert but as well the official presence of D.I. Sutcliffe who had taken my place there.

The door had closed on the three of them. If there were a murmur of voices from within, I didn't want to hear it.

I went downstairs. The front door stood open. Outside, the radiant summer day hit me.

Even if I had wanted to obey Steve's last appeal — and that was unthinkable! — surely now it was too late. Already Willard was welcoming a portly, bespectacled gentleman, who had brought with him a fresh-faced young assistant. They were apologising for missing the road at the junction.

Their vehicle was parked next to Steve's, still waiting there — so near and yet so far, he would be thinking now. Well, hadn't I given him chances enough, done for him far more than I should? . . .

'Mr. Enderby!' I whispered. I kept tugging at his arm like a worrisome child.

* * *

The portly Mr. Leigh-Ferriby eyed me disapprovingly over his glasses. The fresh-faced young man was staring at me. It occurred to me what a crumpled, overwrought, bramble-torn wreck I must look after these past hours — as though that mattered, as though anything did but the echo of Steve's desperate voice.

'One moment, my dear.' Willard tried to wave me politely aside. 'This way, gentlemen! — I think Mrs. Stafford has some refreshments laid on for us . . . Ruth, can't you see I'm busy here?'

We were almost at the front door. My moment was almost gone.

'Bless my soul, what was that?' Mr. Leigh-Ferriby exclaimed. 'Someone up there at that window?'

I had heard a sharp tapping on glass without at first realising where it came from. Looking up, I glimpsed just a swift beckoning gesture.

I struggled for words. Somehow I got them out.

'Mr. Enderby, that's — Ray, he wants to see you. He sent me to tell you!'

This far, no farther, I would deliver the message. Maybe enough to arouse a stab of anxiety in Willard's mind, though he murmured only a casual, 'Very well, when I've a moment.

— We'll use the dining-room, it does at least boast a table and chairs! . . . '

As he guided the legal pair through the new-paint aroma of the big bare hall, he added to me, 'Oh, Ruth, would you please call your mother in?'

I left them there in the panelled room, with a briefcase being opened on the table. But I didn't turn towards the kitchen. I went back upstairs.

The kindest thing I could do for Steve was to end this unendurable situation quickly! So I was fetching Willard to him. But there would be no chance for even the master-brain of the partnership to save them: not if I announced in front of the official witnesses, 'Oh yes, Mr. Enderby, and your stepson specially asked me to say you must 'call off the plan' — and Mr. Sutcliffe happens to be a police officer waiting to hear exactly what that means!'

The landing was deserted, the whole house unnaturally still. But I didn't need to linger long by the closed door of the room where I had left Steve. Rapid steps were mounting the stairs behind me. And this time there was unguarded annoyance in Willard's dismissal, 'Ruth, I asked you to find your mother, will you kindly do that?'

I didn't answer. I opened the door.

The fact that Steve was actually alone struck me first with almost disbelieving dismay — and destroyed my hasty plan of action on the instant. Were they mad, I thought quite wildly, to allow him to signal from the window and leave him here unwatched?

He was still on the window-seat where Alan had planted him. I saw his eyes lift quickly as the door opened.

'Well, it took you long enough! You're too late now!' He said it to Willard, not to me. He didn't even look at me. 'Didn't you guess this whole set-up was a trap, an ambush? — these 'guests' were specially planted? — '

'I've no idea what you mean,' Willard cut him quickly short. 'I'm afraid you don't look very well, perhaps Ruth will fetch you some water?'

I didn't stir. Not because this excuse to get rid of me was so obvious, but my legs had suddenly turned to rubber — made so by one tell-tale glimpse of cold metal.

I saw it, even before Steve thrust out both his hands towards Willard with the violent question, 'Are you blind as well as stupid, you imbecile? — this is what I get for working with you! And you got me into it, now you get me out! — ' He lapsed into a tide of French or Italian or both, as unintelligible as it plainly was abusive.

But there were no words needed. Crudely, the handcuffs told all.

At this chilling moment I felt for Willard — no, not admiration, never that! — but a grudging sort of respect. His face was grey, but he absorbed instantly what must have been a staggering shock. If his partner was going sadly to pieces, he remained even now well in command.

He gave one swift glance back along

the landing, and quickly closed the door. He didn't try again to turn me out — I would be safer here than running to fetch someone. But the glance he gave me was clear enough: 'Congratulations to you!' the steely eyes said.

Nor did he view his stepson any more kindly. Steve was breaking down into weak tears, burying his face in his imprisoned hands, and there was a stern contempt in the way Willard gripped both his shoulders.

'Come on, Raoul! Pull yourself together, can't you? Save the Mediterranean hysterics till later!' There was so little response that Willard shook him, not gently. 'Raoul! Let's have it slowly and in English! Where are they now? How much have they got on you?'

This time there was an answer, broken and muffled. 'They leave me here while they fix things for *you* — they make sure I don't drive my car! And I don't know how much they have — but I know this, you've never paid me all I'm worth to you — ' Suddenly his head lifted, his eyes blazed through their brightness of tears. 'If I'm being locked up for you, I'll tell everything I know! All of it, you hear me?'

'Everyone will, if you carry on this way,' Willard warned. 'Just calm down and listen. I'll help you, of course I will! Keep your mouth shut, and I'll get Herries down here to see you through, you can trust him to look after you.'

'This Herries, this bent pet lawyer of yours — he's all you can offer? And where will you be meanwhile?' his stepson flamed at him. 'You think I'm a fool, I don't know the fortunes waiting for you in foreign banks under different names? You think I'll go through this while you live somewhere in luxury? Well, I won't do it! I won't! If I go to prison you'll come with me, I promise!'

He was openly crying now. I would never forget his hunted face, the last of its bravado fled. I watched him cling to Willard's arm and sob a pitiful plea, 'Don't leave me here! — if you can make a break for it, take me with you! Look, outside is your car, yes? — you smuggle me out, we drive just down the coast — an hour on the Ferry . . . well, do we wait here till everywhere swarms with police? — '

Until this moment I hadn't spoken or moved. But I moved now, to put my back against the door. I wouldn't be shifted without a struggle.

'Steve, I'm sorry. If you try it, I'll scream the place down! Can't you see you'll only make things worse?'

Strangely, Willard came quickly to my support, in a hurry to get this over.

'The girl's right. If we're stopped along the road, would that help either of us? Use your head, boy! They can't make much out of this — maybe not even attempted fraud, with Herries on the job. And our tracks elsewhere are covered too well, *if* you keep quiet about them — that's the truth, Steve! — ' He had switched from the stern 'Raoul' to that familiar name, smoothly coaxing and persuasive. 'Come on, trust me. I won't let you down.'

He was making an impression. Steve asked sullenly, 'Then what is it I have to do?'

'It's very easy. Create a nice big diversion here, something noisy and spectacular — that's child's play for you! — to cover me, give me a chance to get well clear. And then Herries will look after you, we'll keep in touch through him. And later, when you can join me, I'll make it up to you. Mind, so long as you hold your tongue I will!'

The appeal was working. Steve seemed to be wavering. He asked abruptly, 'How much is it worth to keep quiet?'

'Oh, we'll agree on something later — something generous!'

'How generous? Or perhaps I shan't manage to keep so dumb. Say, a bonus on past jobs? Ten per cent minimum?'

I guessed Willard would agree any bribe to get quickly away. I guessed too, he would hesitate about any future partnership with someone not just prone to 'Mediterranean hysterics' but possessed of a mind fully as calculating as his own.

There was creeping up on me as well real alarm as to what would happen to my interfering self now I knew all I did! Would Willard force me to go along with him on his flight? But if this was the time to scream or to run, I could do neither. I stood there watching, listening, turned to stone.

'All right,' Willard was saying shortly, 'there's no time to waste, I'll agree to ten per cent!'

'On everything? Even the Strickland shares thing I almost bungled?'

'Even that! For heaven's sake, do you want it all spelt out? The Pitlake Trust, the railway bonds — '

'Which ones?' still Steve insisted stubbornly.

'On both! Lady Childe's South American ones — and the Australian deal last year. *And* any other jobs you can think of! Now are you satisfied? Mind, you'll have to earn it — but won't it be worth waiting for? — '

Steve said, 'I doubt it.' He said it with sudden quiet, in rather an odd way: he was on his feet now, near the second door in the room — the door ajar between this master-bedroom and its dressing-room, newly papered and bare.

Bare, but not empty. As he pushed the door open wider, incredibly I saw attentive, listening faces. He was asking very composedly, 'Will that do for a start, gentlemen?'

It was the Detective Inspector who answered him.

'Lady Amelia Childe — with an 'e', of course? — we'll be delighted to have some answers to that one! . . . Yes, I think that will do very nicely for a start, Mr. Stevenson!'

7

There were questions, voices, people, so many people. Mr. Sutcliffe seemed to have reinforcements on hand I had known nothing about. I still couldn't realise that all the frantic urgency was suddenly over.

For a while I sat numbed and still on a packing case. Just a few impressions stood out from the blur — foremost, the kind concern of Alan. He stayed close to me, and I clung to him. Briefly too I saw my sister's face, pale but smiling: it was Nina, before she hurried back downstairs, who hugged me hard and whispered, 'Ruth, you were so brave and wonderful!'

'No, I wasn't. I didn't know what he was trying to do. I didn't believe a word he said to me.'

They wouldn't understand, because they were unaware of all that had passed between Steve and me: how he had finally sent me with an open warning to Willard, realising that was the only thing I *would* believe, the only way to gain my help for his startling plan.

Alan said quietly, 'It was all Steve's idea. Sutcliffe just went along with him. He doesn't always follow the conventional book, evidently.'

'He likes playing it by ear,' Robert Collyer agreed. 'He gets results.'

Today the results were in no doubt, evidenced by the face of Willard Enderby suddenly bare of its suave mask, the practised deceiver at last outwitted, out-plotted, beaten. It gave me no sense of triumph to think of it. In any case, the triumph wasn't mine.

I muttered, 'I can't just sit here! I must go to Mum.'

Even the appalling task of breaking the news had been done for me — or so much as could be told all at once to ailing Cecily Stafford. Alan and Nina had explained gently that my fears about 'dear Will' had proved all too well founded. Now she was trying to rest, and Nina and Jonquil were with her.

It was time I joined them. But first I had one thing to do. I went across to Steve, still in his place by the window — and looking down somewhat pensively at two police cars that had nosed in among the other vehicles, to the great interest of the staring housepainters.

Someone had brought him some coffee. I hadn't even thought to do that. As he looked round at me, I said just 'Thank you!' short and sharp.

Alan managed scarcely better. He held out a spontaneous hand, before realising Steve's weren't yet free. I sensed that very telling part of the drama had been part of Steve's plan, his instinct for theatrical effect knowing just how to deal a sufficient jolt to Willard. And it had worked. Rather too well, for now the show was over, no-one present was inclined to reverse that side of it.

It didn't seem to worry him unduly. Alan was by far the more awkward party to their peculiar handshake as he mumbled, 'Sorry it's ending up for you like this.'

'Me too!' the distinctive familiar voice agreed.

'I'm really sorry. It was quite a virtuoso performance you gave just now.'

'Not so bad, was it?' Steve accepted the compliment quite brightly. 'Worth an Oscar, I thought. Of course, I did cheat a bit — I played a similar scene on the stage, I hammed that up too! The only thing is, the hardware they used for 'props' was easier to get rid of afterwards. Oh well, *c'est la vie!*'

Alan was as lost for words as I was. But neither of us needed to say more. Hugh Sutcliffe was coming across with one of his 'reinforcements' to claim 'the star of the show', he said. He apologised, 'Sorry to break this up,' and then looked down quite cordially into Steve's face to ask, 'And how is Raoul?'

They were reproachfully sad eyes that lifted to his.

'Completely desolated. Do you forget, there follows now for you all the glory — and for me all the misery?'

'It's a cruel hard world we live in,' the Inspector agreed gravely. 'I think you'd better come down to the car before you have us all in tears — No, don't worry, not the same car as your stepfather. You'll be doing all the explaining to us, not to him.'

I wondered whether Steve felt any belated pangs of remorse for his betrayal of Willard. I had no delusions that he acted out of tender regard for me, or because I shamed or bullied him into it. His real and only spur would have been the doubts I put in his mind about the death of his adored mother, doubts that might well be eventually disproved. It was as well not to know how much, or how little, he had really cared for me.

As he got to his feet with a resigned

sigh, I turned my head away. I kept it turned.

Alan waited quietly beside me. But when, in a few minutes, we both started downstairs, he said something with an unexpected depth of sensitivity: 'I suppose he's an artist — the kindest thing you can call him — with an ego to match. And he's still playing to the gallery. But this time he'll suddenly find the footlights dark and the audience gone home.'

They were words that would linger with me long after today's wounds had begun to heal.

As yet, they seemed beyond all hope of healing, as I sat by my mother.

'I can't believe it,' she kept repeating. 'I just can't, not of dear W — ' She stopped short each time she reached the name. 'Of course, sometimes I used to wonder what he saw in me. He's so clever and I'm so silly — you know that's true . . . '

It was useless to shake my head, just as it would be to tell her of the others who had been deceived before her — though not all their pain had been her pain, they had trusted Willard with their worldly goods but not all with their hearts. She plunged on in her misery, 'I did wonder, sometimes! But . . . oh, I'll never get over this, and no-one will ever know how I feel . . . '

I saw then what I alone could do for her. I whispered, 'I know. I know exactly. It's really the same for me too.'

Surprised and anxious, she peered at me. 'Because young What's-his-name was in it as well? I can't believe that either! Did you really care for him?'

'Mum, I was taken in far more than you were! I came here especially to rescue you, with my eyes wide open, and what did I do? He said he loved me, and I swallowed every word. I never dreamed it was just part of the plan. He asked me to marry him, I even intended to say 'yes' — '

She breathed, wide-eyed, 'Did you really?'

'Yes. In spite of Alan, in spite of everything.'

'Oh, Ruth,' she whispered. 'I didn't know. Oh, of course, there was something special about him — but darling, I always did feel he wasn't right for you, not seriously. You two are so different! It never would have done, would it?'

I agreed that it wouldn't. This was working, as I had hoped. Her warm concern for me, the fire of her indignation — 'I'd like to give him a piece of my mind!' — was carrying her over the first crushing impact of her own shock.

For my deluded, betrayed sake, there came the tears she hadn't yet shed for her own. I held her in my arms and let her cry them, relieving, loving tears.

'We — we're a pair of idiots, aren't we?' she quavered. 'But we'll show both of them they can't treat us this way! We'll show them we *can* get over it!'

'We'll show them,' I said. My own eyes were stone-dry.

I went on holding her. I hid my face, and my pain, against her rumpled gold hair.

★　★　★

We were on our way back to Sea Winds amazingly soon, due largely to the kind offices of Mr. Sutcliffe. When I tried to tell him my mother just wanted everything to be forgotten and go no further, he smiled at me reassuringly.

'We'll make things as easy for Mrs. Stafford as we can. I'll see you both tomorrow. You've all had a rough time, just get her back to her bed and take care of her. I've plenty to keep me interested meantime.'

'Yes. Please, who is Lady Amelia Childe with an 'e'?'

'Ah. A wealthy but unwise lady who invested in an obscure South American railway — so obscure it doesn't actually exist. She was encouraged to do so by the 'grandson of the Company President'. A smile to die for, she said, fractured English, very persuasive.'

I wished I hadn't asked.

He wanted to know if we needed a lift back. He told my mother, 'You have a very competent and caring family around you, Mrs. Stafford. A lot of blessings to count.'

She answered earnestly, 'I know. Yes, I do know!'

We drove back in Alan's car. The sun was still shining, and shone too on the welcoming white walls of Sea Winds. I had known a stolen happiness here.

We persuaded Mum to lie down, having first swept away Willard's photo from her bedside. We rang the doctor who had recently attended her. I didn't really mind the sensation rippling through the hotel: during her stay she had endeared herself to everyone, and sympathy soon brought to her room flowers and messages, a friendly postcard from the Taylors and an invitation to their home, an evil-looking phial of smelling-salts from old Mrs. Pike.

I was glad she had friends, and would

always have friends. And even before the doctor arrived to help her, two new glimmers of comfort shone in her world.

The first was a brainwave of Alan's, that The Old Lodge could hold real potential as a guest-house. A few conversions and some publicity, and she might be welcoming visitors for 'home from home family holidays'. He waxed quite eloquent, enough to fire her imagination.

'It might be quite fun?' She turned to me doubtfully, and I said at once, 'Lots of fun, Mum! — and lots of very hard work! If you need a manager/chief cook-and-bottle-washer, I'm up for all of it!' Already I pictured her drifting among her guests, chatting brightly while everything was organised for her behind the scenes. Well, it would fill a void, it would keep her from remembering. And I doubted, now, whether I could ever settle down again with Mr. Harding and the City office walls.

That was the first moment of help.

The second was very different.

I had thought myself immune from more shocks. I hadn't counted on seeing my sister, so brave during this shattering day, suddenly succumb to pent-up emotions and make a dive for comforting arms. Not my arms, nor our mother's. They were Alan's that quieted her sobs, that held her so very close.

I knew then, before a word was said. Nina and Alan, two quiet, kind, gentle people, so much together since I began fighting my mother's battles — and hadn't I even asked him, when I first came here, 'You will look after her while I'm away? . . . '

Now, Nina would need no more looking after from me. Alan's bereaved home would find a new loving completeness. Joni would have a mother. How could I blame any of them?

'We didn't know how we could ever tell you!' Nina tried to say. 'Did we, Alan? We tried to pretend it hadn't happened.'

'You can't help how you feel.' I knew

that, if anyone did. 'Don't both look so worried! You'll be very, very happy — and I'll dance at your wedding, I promise!'

The word 'wedding' didn't upset my mother too much. She had whispered to me one shocked and feeling 'My poor, poor Ruth!' — but was soon swept into a fervour of anticipation. Such a perfect bride Nina would make! And they must go somewhere wonderful for the honeymoon, as part of her wedding-gift. And Joni could stay with her new Grandma while they were away.

'I'll have a dress made at Madame Xenia's, that pretty heliotrope shade,' she pondered drowsily. She was still holding my hand when the others had left. 'Ruth, do you mind terribly?'

'I've no right to mind, have I? And they'll be very happy. They deserve to be.'

'And so do you,' she whispered. The grip of her hand tightened, she looked quickly away from the space where that photograph had stood. 'We've just each other left now, haven't we? Well, that'll be enough!' A brief defiance glimmered into her tired eyes, she repeated again our pact made in the depth of today's mortal hurt. 'We'll show them all, Ruthie. We'll show them!'

Presently, I left her a short while to go downstairs, where everyone was very kind. I talked to Alan, he and I alone. Perhaps I had never been sure if it were love we shared or a dear, deep friendship. Now, when he tried to thank me for helping him through the dark time of his bereavement, I stopped him quickly.

If ever I needed him, he would be my brother, my friend. 'Many blessings left to count,' hadn't my mother been told? I would never let his future be clouded by any regrets of mine that I had finally lost this man who could have been my life and my all.

'But, Nina,' I had to ask her, 'I got it all wrong, but I did imagine you'd fallen for — '

'For Steve?' She looked quite aghast. 'Not seriously! Only like — a poor little bird sort of hypnotised by a snake!'

Was it too unkind? It tore anew into a raw wound.

I talked to Jonquil, only her questions weren't easy to answer. I reassured my mother's friends as best I could. In the evening of that endless day I was back in her shaded bedroom, watching as she finally dropped asleep. I wished I could sleep too, but my eyes were wide open, my ears caught at once a soft tap on the door.

Alan whispered, 'Robert just phoned with a message.'

'Mum's asleep. I can't wake her.'

'No, the message is for you. Steve wants to see you.'

I clung to the door as though it were an anchor. 'No! Definitely, no! I've nothing left to say to him.'

'But maybe we owe it to him? I can drive you over there now,' Alan insisted. 'Nina will sit in here while we're gone.'

I had found out today he could be

very firm. Still I protested, all the way to his car, more and more along the way. My nerves would stand no more. My mother would wake and miss me. 'Anyway,' I said almost hopefully, 'how do you know they'll even let me see him?'

'They will,' Alan assured me. It was all very well his suddenly turning so masterful. This time he should mind his own business!

He was driving along the streets of this town where once or twice I had shopped with Mum, mostly closed up now and quiet. He parked in his careful way. Sunlight was dying on the rooftops, evening birdsong murmured. He took me through the entrance of quite a sizeable red-brick building.

I was cold almost to the point of faintness. Well, I was here — if I owed that much! Out of a mist I heard Robert Collyer's precise voice, so he was still around too. There was some kind of reception area with a counter, official uniforms, the flicker of a computer screen. 'Will you come this way, Miss Stafford?' one of the uniforms was saying.

And then Alan was left behind. I saw a passageway to some sort of office, then another door, another room. A table and some chairs . . . and a metal grille across the window.

Where he sat at the table the light was full on his face, emphasising the tiredness round those dark, alert eyes. Not even so alert any more, only subdued and defeated.

I thought of Alan's words, the audience gone home, the footlights turned out. Here in this bare barred room they were.

★   ★   ★

I wouldn't sit down, stiffly standing to attention. I realised we were actually being left alone: virtually alone, though the door to the adjoining office stood wide open. I said gruffly, 'Well, I'm here! What do you want?'

Only for an instant he looked up at me. But his voice was the same as it had ever been.

'I'm so sorry to drag you here. Thank you for coming. Is your mother — ?'

'Mum is a much stronger person than she looks. She'll survive. She even asked me tonight to sell her engagement ring for charity — so I'm just hoping it won't turn out to be glass, do you happen to know — ?'

'I bought it myself from the Barron Jewellers in London. It's genuine.'

'I'm glad to hear it! She'll be fine in a while, we both shall — and even better when we open up The Old Lodge as a b & b guest-house, that'll keep us both very busy. But I'm sure you're not interested in that.'

'It sounds like a great idea. I'm really glad for you.'

'Are you?'

'Of course. Ruth — ' The way he said my name, just the same. 'I shouldn't have asked you to leave her and come here — '

'You've said that! And it doesn't matter, I wanted a chance to thank you again. I'd have written it to you anyway. Can we please just hurry and get this over?'

'It won't take long. I want just to tell a little story to you. Here I've been telling lots of them and signing my name to them — but this one I want you to hear before we say goodbye.'

I muttered, 'We've said goodbye!' There was simply no point in my standing here listening. Very discouragingly, I looked at my watch. But he didn't hurry, leaning forward with his hands clasped quietly on the table. The self-possession (or should you call it effrontery?) that had so shattered Alan this morning was more lacking now than I had ever known it as he searched for words.

Not that his 'story' began very originally. I had heard the beginning before, the childhood full of moves and partings, later the lonely young man mourning the loss of the idolised mother whose love had fitfully lighted his unstable world.

But I hadn't known before that after the shock of her sudden death he had some kind of total collapse. There had just come his way a major role in a new play, by far his best chance yet of stardom — to his mother's huge delight, and on the last night of her life they had celebrated it together. But subsequently he walked out in the middle of the opening night, overcome by grief and a complete loss of self-belief.

At this lowest of ebbs he was driven to ask help from Willard Enderby, the stepfather almost a stranger to him, to pay off the not inconsiderable debts he had run up: and Willard did more than that, taking him off to a quiet retreat in the Swiss mountains to coax, nurse, bully him back from the black depths his emotional, volatile nature couldn't cope with. However, Willard wasn't really a saviour in time of need. He had realised how useful these quick wits and an uncanny skill in playing parts might be to him.

For favours asked and received he demanded assistance in return, maybe to begin with just a phone call in some persuasive foreign voice to aid a 'business transaction' — and that was the start of a slippery slope. If there were needed a Bolivian mining technician, a French wine expert, a Swiss banker — all of those were now conveniently to hand, in one talented individual who owed a favour.

Was it too hard to understand how the sheer thrill of adventure appealed to that devil-may-care streak so inherent in Steve — and his indebtedness to Willard, along with the lack of sane counsel and a steady background, had done the rest? Was it even so hard to see how he took an artist's pride in each performance, so obscuring the dark implications beneath?

And it was so wicked and pitiful a waste! You could say he had been led astray at a time of grief and weakness:

that was true, but time had gone by since then. If much of the blame lay with Willard, his young partner had a mind plenty strong enough to say 'No!', to refuse any further prostituting of his inborn gifts.

Tonight, it was far too late for tardy regret and remorse. The clock couldn't be turned back. If he sought from me now one word of comfort, what could I find to say?

'I'm glad you told me. And I'm truly grateful for what you did for Mum today, it took a lot of courage.' The words came out still abrupt and hard. 'I — I hope things won't be too bad for you.'

'It's not important. I don't much care.'

'Well, you should care. You've a wonderful talent, one day you'll make better use of it. People will queue for miles at stage doors for your autograph, you'll see!'

It brought no faintest glimmer of interest to his face. He seemed suddenly anxious to be rid of me, asking, 'Is Alan waiting for you?'

'Yes. And Mum will be worrying. I'd better go.'

There was nothing to keep me. I didn't say the word 'goodbye', but he said it softly for me as I turned away to the office door and freedom.

'Goodbye. I'll always remember you, Ruth. I'll always — love you with my heart and my soul . . . '

So very low those last words that I was at the door before I understood them. And even then I wasn't sure, I faltered, 'Did you say — ?'

'I've always loved you. Since the day I met you. That was never, never a lie.'

There had been such a tangled web of lies. He had even been paid to tell me words of love on summer beaches, in twilight gardens! Only now there were no roses, not a shadow of one.

'It was the very first time I saw you. In the hotel dining-room, you were so lost and worried, you remember that? *'The sad heart of Ruth . . . '*'

I whispered, ' 'She stood in tears amid the alien corn' . . . but you said it was 'cornflakes' instead.' Yes, I remembered. Dear heaven, I remembered!

'I loved you even then. The more I came to know you, I loved you more and more each day. Oh, such fights I had with Willard, begging and begging him to leave you and your family in peace! — you saw one of those battles — yes? — the night of the big thunderstorm? . . . So then I wanted only for us to go away together, leave it all behind us! Because — ' Now his voice was shaking. 'Because I saw no *danger* for your mother, I didn't know she was sick. I thought she would be happy with her Mr. Wonderful, the money no loss to her. But I wanted no more part of him, no more of his schemes, not ever, not ever! I swore I would start a new life, to live it this time only for you . . . '

His face was half averted. Gradually I had crept back across the room, and he turned away from me still further.

'Don't stand there, just go! Go away and don't look back! You know all of everything now, but I don't expect you to believe any of it. You've wasted too much time here, your mother she waits for you — '

My mother, she waited. Alan's car, it waited too. Still I didn't move.

'Ruth! Did you hear me?' He said it angrily now. 'Get out of this miserable place, forget you ever came here!'

'You've really loved me all this time?'

'Haven't I just said so? Which is more reason for doubting, but it's true, I swear to you by all the stars that shine in heaven! Now will you please, please just *go* — or shall I walk out of here myself? — '

'You can try,' I said unfairly. 'How far do you think you'll get?'

We were two very different people, my mother had so wisely said. His world had never been mine, so few of his thoughts were my thoughts. Yet always, always I had loved him, when I understood him least, abhorred most what I feared he might be doing. When he hurt me more than anyone ever had hurt me, still beyond all reason that love had survived. So how could I stop loving him now? Now, when finally I had come to know him so well?

Surely, what we shared was too precious to be lost? He had proved today his true love for me, if not in this morning's high drama, here now even more. In all his lonely need he was trying to send me away, to make this our final parting, because he feared I would be hurt still more.

I said, 'Look at me! — will you just look at me?' And at last his eyes lifted straight into mine, I saw the soul beyond them desolate and regretting and longing. 'I love you too. And that means for always, whatever trouble you're in, whatever people think . . . No, keep looking at me,' I had to plead again. 'This won't be for ever. We'll get through this awful time somehow. Steve, do you remember I promised to give you an answer today, whether I'd marry you? I still can't quite square up all you've told me and those things you did, maybe I never shall . . . but if — if the offer's still open — ?'

I paused there. I drew a deep breath.

'Do you want the answer now? It's yes, I'll be Mrs. Stevenson. Like you said to me, today, tomorrow, anywhere, any time! . . . Is that the answer you wanted? . . . '

Somehow I had his hands in mine, and felt how desperately they clung to me, with a chill that neither my words nor my touch could warm. Nor was the brightness in his eyes really anger, but the sudden flooding of silent tears. I whispered, 'Well, this is more up to your usual standards . . . '

Yet the moment of breakdown, now it had come, was strangely devoid of flamboyant drama. He bowed his dark head straight down on the table. I heard him sob, once, twice — only quietly, very quietly, like a spent child.

There were voices in the adjoining room, steps along the passage. We weren't even alone, enquiring eyes observing us from the inner doorway. Indeed, a bleak place, a bizarre manner, to pledge our love and loyalty. But there would be better times, other places.

I bent my head down close beside his. I held him fast in my love and sorrow and hope. I closed my eyes upon all I didn't want to see.

★ ★ ★

Welcoming lights were shining in the hotel windows. A belated gull or two wheeled overhead, this eternal day waning finally to its close. It seemed I had been away from here half a lifetime.

I knew Alan had already phoned them, but I wasn't sure how much he had said. He drove me back almost in silence, no doubt aware I wasn't able to talk coherently. Now, I found them all waiting for me in my mother's room. She was wide awake, propped up in bed with a supper tray, a cardigan around her shoulders.

Today had aged her. I couldn't avoid seeing that.

They made room for me beside her. Joni was drowsily working her way through a luridly pink milk-shake, blissful at staying here overnight, more blissful because no-one had sent her to bed. Nina poured me some tea. They said I looked tired, but I wasn't tired any more.

'Auntie Ruth,' Joni accused, 'you didn't bring him back with you!'

I wasn't sure how much the child understood. Alan came quietly to my rescue, 'He's a bit busy at present. Mind you don't spill that drink on the carpet!'

'Ruthie,' my mother whispered beside me, and I looked into her anxious face. 'I just don't know what to say to you, except — are you really sure you know what you're doing?'

'I'm sure. And we worked it all out together, Mum. I'll stay with you till The Old Lodge is up and running, for as long as you want! — '

She stopped me, 'Didn't Alan tell you? — he and Nina will move near here to help with the guest-house idea. Alan can commute to town. It'll do Joni a world of good to live away from London!'

It would, of course. It would be a happy, busy future for all of them. I said not very steadily, 'I'm very glad for you. I just want you to know — Steve wants me to tell you — he's desperately sorry . . . and he hates the idea of bringing disgrace to the family, 'burdening us all with a criminal,' that's what he said. So — he won't marry me unless you can accept it — and manage to forgive him, I know that's almost too much to ask. Please don't worry about it, Mum. Whatever you want, we'll understand.'

Indeed, who could expect her to forgive so much, to welcome — or even just painfully tolerate — this intruder into her secure circle? I still went on, because it must be said, 'We want you to think about it when you feel you can. Whatever you say, we'll agree to do.'

Then I whispered, because only she and I knew of the deep bond we forged in our mutual pain, 'It can still be just the two of us. He knows, he wouldn't have it any other way.'

Again she stopped me. This time, her blue eyes were misted.

'Well, I've been thinking it over already, ever since Alan phoned us . . . which was a shock, I don't mind saying. My dear, I'll never be able to repay all you've done for me — it's true, don't shake your head! And if there's anything or anyone in this world you really want, do you think I could say 'no'? But if — if he — '

'You can say it. If he ends up with a prison sentence, I'll just have to wait for him, for as long as it takes. He'll need me.'

She reached over to squeeze my arm. 'It's all so sad. But I suppose if you two still care so much for each other after all you've been through, that must mean something. And I do realise he could have saved his own skin today if he chose! It's your future that worries me so much. But maybe there's something I can do about a settled future for — for — oh dear, *what* do I have to call him now? — '

I prompted, 'Steve.' But she had her own ideas about that too.

'No, no! It's 'Raoul', isn't it? Such a beautiful, romantic name — and wasn't I right about the Mediterranean eyes? — so that's what he'll be in this family! . . . Listen, Alan and Nina will help me all they can, but they'll have their own lives to live — and with this silly dicky heart of mine I mustn't work too much — so *someone* needs to take this hotel idea in hand and do all the hard work and make it succeed! We know he's been a bad lad, but he's young, he has lots of time to turn things around if he really wants to . . . '

She paused to gulp in breath. The next words, when they came, were almost beyond my believing.

'This is my idea, Ruthie. You two could take on The Old Lodge together!

How about that?' She added, with just a glimmer of her pretty smile, 'Anyway, aren't the Continentals wonderful hoteliers?'

I was very near to breaking down. I tried to say, 'Would you really trust him that much?' — but my voice failed utterly. Only an hour ago I had insisted to Steve that Cecily Stafford had great hidden strength of character. Little had I dreamed it was as great as this.

For the moment, the tears in my eyes were her answer. Later, when we were alone, I would tell her all that was in my heart.

'I suppose really I'm a lucky woman,' she was rambling on, 'like that nice Mr. Sutcliffe said. With the 'hotel' to look forward to, and all of you so anxious to help me — and a ready-made poppet of a grand-daughter . . . ' She smiled across at Joni, who had finally fallen asleep: and the fondness of her glance towards Joni's father, already so completely one of the family, made me flinch a little. She murmured as though

I had said it aloud, 'I know. And if your Ray — I mean, Raoul — proves to me he's worthy of all your belief in him, he'll be one of us too. That's all I ask of him.'

If she sighed momentarily, remembering another man she had been so ready to trust with herself and her all, who amongst us would breathe the name of Willard Enderby? She went on earnestly, 'Ruth, of course he's got to take his punishment, but maybe they'll let him off a bit lightly after he practically did those policemen's jobs for them?'

Alan said gravely, 'Don't count on that, Mrs. Stafford. But Robert did say to me, there may be some slight grounds for very cautious optimism.' Unconsciously he mimicked his friend's precise manner. 'So possibly, — er, Steve — er — '

'Raoul,' my mother said firmly. 'Let's hope he's right, dear.'

I knew that when Robert Collyer conceded 'cautious optimism', other people flung their hats in the air. I knew too there must be an agonising wait before the darkness of today and tomorrow gave way to another tomorrow. But day and night I would hope and pray.

I was hoping and praying now as I looked round the circle of faces, this dear family of mine and those who would soon join it. I was proud to be one of them, of the loving help they had given me today — and would give the man I loved, I was sure they would, for my sake.

Tonight my hands weren't empty, with the touch of his still so real and near. Still I could hear the parting words we said. Not even a very sad farewell — for was any parting too grievous, when so nearly we had parted for always? I had even teased him, 'Please, no tears, no flowery orations! Haven't we had enough of your terrible over-the-top melodramas for one day?'

There wasn't even a shadow of his unforgettable smile, the smile of a stranger that had conquered my heart.

But the smile was in his whispered words.

'But today has been a very special day. The day Raoul has Seen The Light . . . '

I read the warmth of devotion in those black, speaking, loving eyes. I heard more words, very simple words.

'I saw the light, dearest angel. When I found you.'

THE END

We do hope that you have enjoyed reading this large print book.

Did you know that all of our titles are available for purchase?

We publish a wide range of high quality large print books including:
Romances, Mysteries, Classics
General Fiction
Non Fiction and Westerns

Special interest titles available in large print are:
The Little Oxford Dictionary
Music Book, Song Book
Hymn Book, Service Book

Also available from us courtesy of Oxford University Press:
Young Readers' Dictionary
(large print edition)
Young Readers' Thesaurus
(large print edition)

For further information or a free brochure, please contact us at:
Ulverscroft Large Print Books Ltd.,
The Green, Bradgate Road, Anstey,
Leicester, LE7 7FU, England.
Tel: (00 44) **0116 236 4325**
Fax: (00 44) **0116 234 0205**

SEASONS OF CHANGE

Margaret McDonagh

When Kathleen Fitzgerald left Ireland twenty years ago, she never planned to return. In England she married firefighter Daniel Jackson and settled down to raise their family. However, when Dan is injured in the line of duty, events have a ripple effect, bringing challenges and new directions to the lives of Dan, Kathleen and their children, as well as Kathleen's parents and her brother, Stephen. How will the members of this extended family cope with their season of change?

CHERRY BLOSSOM LOVE

Maysie Greig

Beth was in love with her boss, but he could only dream of the brief passionate interlude he had shared with a Japanese girl long ago, and of the child he had never seen. Beth agrees to accompany him to Japan in search of his daughter. There perhaps, the ghost of Madame Butterfly would be laid, and he would turn to her for solace . . . Her loyal heart is lead along dark and dangerous paths before finding the love she craves.

THE SEABRIGHT SHADOWS

Valerie Holmes

Elizabeth, bound to a marriage she wants no part in, is strong willed and determined to free herself from the arrangement her father Silas has made. But she is trapped. The family's fortunes are linked to and dependent upon her marriage to Mr Timothy Granger, a man she despises. It takes a bold act of courage and the interference of her Aunt Jessica to make her see the future in a different light and save the family from ruin.

THE TWO OF US

Jennifer Ames

When Mark Dexter, visiting Australia, invited Janet to work in his publishing house in the United States, she thought he was offering her heaven. They had an adventurous and thrilling trip by plane to New York, lingering in Fiji and Havana; but when they reached New York Janet found she could not get away from Julian Gaden, an odd character whom Mark had introduced her to in a Sydney night club . . .

JANIE

Iain Torr

Janie is a champion skier. Young and beautiful, she is continually in the news, while Roy is a struggling writer, obscure and lonely. He falls in love with her, but realises that she is far above him. Then, abruptly, the situation changes. Janie suffers an accident and slips out of the news, but Roy makes the headlines when the film rights of one of his books are sold . . . Can Janie and Roy overcome their differences and find lasting happiness?

PHOENIX IN THE ASHES

Georgina Ferrand

Paul Varonne had been dead for six months, yet at Château Varonne reminders of him were still evident. Living there was his mother, who still believed him alive and Chantal, his amoral cousin. Into this brooding atmosphere comes Paul's widow, Francesca, after a nervous breakdown. When she meets Peter Devlin, an Englishman staying in the village, it seems that happiness is within her grasp — until she learns the staggering truth about the château and its inhabitants.